# ISLAND OF MISFITS

by Robert Rahula

## ALSO BY ROBERT RAHULA

*NOVELS:*
*Messieurs*
*Panamaniac*
*Day Another Paradise In*
*One Last Fling*
*Bathhouse Stories*
*All the Yage in Reno*
*Exigent Circumstances*
*A Small Summation of Things*
*Conversation in a Belgian Bar*
*Uninvited Guest*
*A Modest Summation of Things*


*POETRY:*
*Trigger Points*
*Dentro Del Corazón Bloqueada*
*Camino*
*Migration*
*I Sing the Body Politic*
*Wonderland*
*From Whose Bourn*
*Poemas Españoles*
*Expat Poems*


*ANTHOLOGIES:*
*Half Life*
*The Essential Dan Landes*
*Horror Stories For Children*

Island of Misfits

© 2015 Robert Rahula

www.robertrahula.com

This is a work of fiction. Characters, organizations, businesses, products, locales, and events portrayed in this book either are products of the author's imagination or are used fictitiously.

First Printing, 2019

ISBN 978-1-7329708-1-6

Alma-Gator Press

Barcelona • Madrid • La Chorrera

dedicated to Alison Wonderland

*To live is the rarest thing in the world. Most people exist, that is all.*

-Oscar Wilde

# Chapter 1:   Island of Misfits

How Ricardo came to reside at the Island of Misfits is another story. But that was the name that Alison had given the two-story, ten-unit apartment building that housed that group of broken, renegade, strange, outlandish and useless expats, including Ricardo. She had only visited once, and Ricardo had to walk her past the group of men sitting outside at the patio picnic table drinking under the palm tree—because if there's one thing expats always do, it's get together and drink—in order to get her into his apartment. The men (and there were only men living at the apartment building) all gawked at Alison as she and Ricardo walked by. They weren't used to seeing women there except for the Panamanian prostitutes some occasionally brought back from town. But Alison was clearly a gringa, and not dressed like a prostitute. Ricardo waved to them, but kept one hand on Alison's arm as he steered her toward his apartment. She had had a long flight into Panama, and Ricardo wanted to get one fuck in before she went to sleep.

"What a group of misfits," she said as she got undressed.
"Yeah, they're pretty odd."
"This whole place is odd... it's a whole island of misfits in this town."

She was right. Villa Rosario was a quiet town, a few miles outside of La Chorrera, just over an hour from Panama City. The town was a typical Panamanian rural town with a Catholic church overlooking a central park. On Saturdays the farmers would set up stalls in the park to sell fruits and vegetables. There were a couple of small restaurants and several bars, one bank and a bus stop. Life was slow and tranquil. Ricardo liked it because there weren't many gringos here. Ironically, he ended up living in the only apartment building in town that housed gringos, because it was the only place he could find that had internet.

"I suppose you want sex," Alison said.

"I do."

"Okay. But let me take a shower first."

While she was showering, Ricardo reflected on what she had said. It was true: all of the men here were misfits in one way of the other. He mentally ran through the faces of the tenants, one by one. Each of them, with the exception of Dan, was over sixty; some were in their seventies. Some were mentally deficient, some were deviant, some were clearly out of their element, and some bordered on being criminal. The one thing they had in common was that they had all somehow managed to scrape together enough money during their lives to retire here. But despite what the retirement guidebooks said, Panama was not really a cheaper place to live than the States. In fact, given the amount of alcohol, drugs, and hookers that some of the residents ran through, it was probably more expensive to live down here.

Ricardo was sitting on the bed still thinking about the various residents when Alison stepped out of the shower.

She stood there naked and asked, "Do you have a clean towel?"

"Oh, yeah. Sorry." He grabbed a towel from the top of the bookshelf that served as his dresser. Alison stood there in front of him, drying herself. Ricardo watched her rub the beads of water off her breasts, her stomach, and in between her legs. There is nothing quite as erotic as the sight of a naked woman drying herself after bathing. Maybe that's why there are so many classic paintings about it. Ricardo started to anticipate running his hands, mouth, and tongue over that beautiful body.

"What were you so deep in thought about?" she asked.

"About what you said, about this place being full of misfits."

"Oh," she replied, "and here I was thinking that you were thinking about me."

Ricardo laughed. "I'm always thinking of *you*, dear." That was one thing about Alison: she knew she was beautiful.

"You ought to write about them," she said

"About who?"

"About those men."

"Hmmm, maybe I will."

"But right now, why don't you come and fuck me," she said.

She tossed the towel over the back of a chair, and walked over to the bed where Ricardo was sitting, pushed him aside, pulled the covers back and laid down, with her legs slightly spread.

"A su servicio," Ricardo said, and started to unbutton his shirt.

# Chapter 2:   Later

It was about a week after Alison had left and returned to New Mexico that Ricardo started to think about her suggestion to write about the Island of Misfits. By then he had been living at the apartment building for a few months and had gotten to know a little about each resident. He had no particular reason to write about them, but on the other hand, he wasn't writing about anything else. His last book was selling reasonably well in the States, and he knew his publisher wouldn't start pressuring him for another book for at least three months. And while he had told his publisher and his friends that he was taking a "vacation" for a while to celebrate the latest publication, the fact was that unless Ricardo was writing, he felt antsy and out-of-sorts. At the moment he didn't have any ideas for a new book, and he hoped that maybe the act of getting descriptions of these people down on paper might help prime the creative pumps. Besides, since Alison was gone, he had nothing else to do. Sex with Alison had left him disorganized. He was always at loose ends after spending any extended time with a lover. It was as if the sex not only left him totally relaxed, but also drained his brain of any ability to focus, plan or carry out any sequence of activities. Alison had stayed two weeks with Ricardo, long enough for them to visit the beaches, spend a few days in Panama City, see the sights, and dine in some nice restaurants, but mostly to stay in bed together and make love. She was simply the most feral woman he had ever met, and was as unabashedly fond of sex as Ricardo was.

For several days after dropping her off at the airport, he felt completely lost, and stayed in his apartment just sleeping or watching mindless TV. He had to break out of this fog, so on the sixth day after she left, he brewed a large pot of coffee, sat down at his desk with his computer, and started to write.

# Chapter 3:  Gregg

Ricardo lived on the first floor, in the next-to-last apartment. Paul lived in the end apartment, to Ricardo's right. On Ricardo's left was the apartment where Gregg lived. Gregg was the Island's resident gay predator, and seemed to know everyone in town, even though he had only been at the Island for a few months. He was in his mid-sixties, with grayish hair and beard, but still slim. And he possessed a certain boyish charm, which Ricardo eventually came to believe was carefully cultivated. He had an outgoing, friendly, chatty personality, engaging in small talk with almost everyone he met, even though his Spanish was minimal. He seemed like a harmless talkative older retired American, until you watched him for a while and saw that his daily ventures downtown in Villa Rosario or over in La Chorrera, into the parks and the restaurants, was really a relentless search for young men. And he invariably found them, not because the young men were gay, but because they were desperately poor. He'd spot some eighteen-year-old without shoes and offer, in an innocent-sounding way, to take him shopping for a pair of shoes. Gregg justified this to Ricardo once by saying, "I'm simply trying to share my good fortune." But during said shopping trip, Gregg would vet the lad, to find out whether he was homeless or living with his family. The shopping trip would be followed by a dinner invitation to Gregg's apartment, where the actual seduction would take place.

Ricardo didn't know all this when he first moved to the Island of Misfits, of course. Gregg just seemed like an outgoing older gay man who introduced himself the day that Ricardo moved in and offered to show him around the town. Even though Ricardo was somewhat familiar with Villa Rosario, he accepted the offer, and after the walking tour they ended up having dinner together at a small outdoor restaurant downtown. It was during that dinner that Gregg mentioned off-handedly that he was gay. The information didn't surprise Ricardo, but something about the timing of it did. It was a sentence that just didn't fit into the context of what they were talking about, and Ricardo had the distinct impression that Gregg had an ulterior motive. They had been talking about Paul, one of the other neighbors in the building.

"Paul kind of keeps to himself," Gregg was saying. "He goes into Panama City a lot on the weekends. But during the week he just stays inside his apartment and watches TV. Although I have seen him bring several different prostitutes to his apartment. At least I assume they were prostitutes by the way they looked."

Ricardo knew from his own experience that Villa Rosario had a few prostitutes and that there were plenty more in the nearby city of La Chorrera. But he didn't want to let that on to Gregg since he had just met him, so he said, "Really? I wouldn't think a town this small would have hookers."

"Oh, no!" Gregg proclaimed. "He drives up to Panama City and brings them here. I don't mind, of course. What everyone does is their own business. I'm not interested in prostitutes, of course, because I'm gay. But whatever Paul wants to do is fine with me. Live and let live, I say."

Something about this conversation nagged at Ricardo. In the first place, Ricardo had intuited immediately upon meeting Gregg that he was gay. So he didn't need to be told. And Ricardo could tell that Gregg wasn't hitting on him, so why bring up the subject of gayness? It was Gregg who had steered the conversation to Paul, and Gregg who had brought up the subject of prostitutes, and then immediately contrasted that by saying he was gay, as if the two facts were opposites. All this was done under the political context of "everyone having a right to do their own thing". Also, Gregg's confident assertion that Paul brought prostitutes in from Panama City was illogical. Ricardo knew Panama City well, and most of the prostitutes who worked there worked out of brothels. There would be no need to drive over an hour there to bring one back to Villa Rosario. Besides, if one was going to bring a prostitute over for an extended visit, one would only need to go to La Chorrera. That night, however, Ricardo let the discussion slide without commenting either way. But, by the time Ricardo saw Gregg in action with Luciano, about two weeks later, Ricardo had already concluded that Gregg's motive that first night was purely political. He had been probing Ricardo to determine whether Ricardo was going to be a friend, foe, or possibly an accomplice to Gregg's pursuit of young men.

That encounter two weeks later happened at the Island's picnic table under the palm tree in the garden, where Ricardo saw Gregg sitting one morning, drinking coffee. At night, that table served as the apartment's gathering spot for drinking beer. In the mornings, however, some of the residents would occasionally sit there with their coffee and enjoy the cool breeze before the day got hot. Ricardo had just emerged from his apartment on an errand to go to the bank when Gregg waved him over. Sitting next to Gregg was a young lad who looked about seventeen or eighteen.

"Ricardo, this is Luciano. He doesn't speak English," Gregg said. Gregg then looked at Luciano and pointed to Ricardo. "Luciano, él ... es ... Ricardo ... Ricardo."

Luciano extended his hand.

"Mucho gusto conocerlo," Ricardo said, shaking Luciano's hand.

Luciano smiled at Ricardo's Spanish. "Igualmente," he said.

"I didn't know you spoke Spanish," Gregg exclaimed. "That's great. You can help me translate some things to

17

Luciano."

Ricardo sat down across from Gregg and Luciano and listened while Gregg explained that he had met Luciano in La Chorrera a few nights before and noticed that Luciano was in a lot of pain. Gregg claimed that Luciano was sitting in the park holding his jaw. "Clearly, there was some sort of dental problem," Gregg explained. Gregg went on to describe how he had taken Luciano to a local dentist in Villa Rosario who had examined him and discovered there was an impacted wisdom tooth plus four cavities in other teeth.

"So the dentist pulled the wisdom tooth yesterday and he's going to fill the four cavities next Monday."

"Uh huh," Ricardo said, listening.

"I'm letting Luciano stay at my place while this dental work is being done."

"Uh huh... why?" Ricardo asked.

"Well, he lives in La Chorrera and he doesn't have bus money to get back and forth," Gregg explained.

Ricardo looked over at Luciano, who was checking his messages on a cell phone.

"Uh huh. Does he have family in La Chorrera?" Ricardo asked.

"No," Gregg said. "His family is in Panama City, but they are kind of estranged. He stays in an apartment with several other boys in La Chorrera," Gregg went on. "He was in such obvious pain when I met him. I asked him the best I could why he hadn't taken care of the problem, and he told me that he didn't have any money. I felt I had to help him."

"I thought everyone was covered by the health system down here," Ricardo said.

"Well, maybe not dental?" Gregg responded.

Ricardo thought about this for a minute and then turned to Luciano and asked, "Por qué usted no tiene seguro de salud?" asking why he didn't have health insurance through the universal health care provided by the government in Panama.

"Porque yo no tengo un trabajo," Luciano explained.

"No he trabajado por dos años. Para obtener un seguro de salud, un trabajador debe pagar cada mes a la caja."

"Por qué no compra usted seguro?" Ricardo asked

"Porque no tengo dinero."

"Pero, es barato, no?"

"Sí, pero no tengo ningún dinero."

"What did he say?" Gregg asked.

"I asked him why he didn't have health coverage, and he said that he hasn't had a job for two years. Down here, you see, you get healthcare automatically when you work, because your employer pays, and a small amount is deducted automatically from your paycheck. If you don't work, you can still get healthcare. It's real cheap if you're out of work, but he said he didn't have any money at all."

"See?" Gregg exclaimed. "He had no way to get his teeth fixed!"

"Uh huh. Why is he estranged from his family? Family is everything down here."

"I'm not sure," Gregg said, "Something about a fight with his father. His father threw him out of the house and had him arrested."

"Really?"

Ricardo took a long look at Luciano, who was busy typing away on his cell phone. He was tall for a Panamanian. Thin, but not starving. What Ricardo would describe as scrappy, but with a handsome face. Ricardo noticed a small stud earring in each ear and a tattoo on his right forearm.

"How old is he?" Ricardo asked

"Twenty-three."

"Hmmm, he looks eighteen. Is he gay?"

"No."

Probably not gay, Ricardo thought. But Ricardo also knew that all of the apartments in the Island were studio apartments, consisting of one room with a bed and a few chairs, a small kitchenette and a bathroom. If Luciano stayed at Gregg's he would have to sleep in the same bed as Gregg.

"So he's staying here with you?" Ricardo asked.

Gregg's response was a little too quick. "Yes, but there's nothing sexual. I've had many friends stay with me—straight friends—where there was only one bed. He just has to put up with my snoring, that's all. I brought him here the other night so he wouldn't miss his dentist appointment yesterday."

Ricardo thought about the situation for a minute. It just didn't ring true. The bus fare from La Chorrera to Villa Rosario was about ninety cents and the bus ran every half hour. Gregg could have given him a couple of dollars for bus fare.

"Are you sure that's safe, Gregg? I mean, how much do you *really* know about him?" Ricardo asked.

"Oh, I vetted him carefully. I used Google Translate and asked him all about his family, his friends, his schooling... I feel he was completely honest with me. I mean, he didn't have to tell me about his criminal convictions..."

"He has convictions?" Ricardo interrupted.

"Well, from the fight with his father, and a few other scrapes on the street. You know, it's tough being homeless."

"I thought he was living with friends."

"Well, he has a couch he sleeps on in La Chorrera, but it's not a good situation. Anyway, can you tell him that we have to go to the pharmacy now to get his antibiotics? We've used up the samples that the dentist gave us."

Ricardo started to tell Luciano, but Gregg interrupted him.

"And ask him if he's hungry. If he is, tell him we'll get something downtown after we go to the pharmacy."

Ricardo translated the message. Luciano nodded his head eagerly, and said yes, he was very hungry.

"Oh good," Gregg said, standing up. "Do you want to grab a bite with us?" Gregg asked Ricardo.

"No thanks, I've already eaten. But I was on my way to the bank. I'll walk with you downtown."

As the three men walked downtown, Gregg chatted on about Luciano, painting a picture of an unfortunate young man who had a rough relationship with his father that resulted in him being thrown out helpless on the street, and how Gregg was simply doing the right thing by paying for this necessary dental care.

"The boy was in such pain, Ricardo. I felt so bad for him. I think I did what anyone would have done."

Ricardo listened, nodding his head, but not commenting. Ricardo knew how Panama's health system worked. Luciano could have gone to any emergency room and they would have arranged for the dental work. If Luciano had no insurance or couldn't pay for the work, the fee would be added onto his national account. Panama has a "dunning" system when it comes to health care. No one is denied emergency health care because they're unemployed. But the fee is tracked, and whenever that person gets a job, the employer must report the new hire to the government, and then that person's paycheck is debited small amounts every month until the fee is paid back.

Of course, it was also true that had Luciano gone to the emergency room, he might have had to wait a week or two for the dental appointment and he would have had to suffer for that time. For that reason, Ricardo decided that Gregg's paying for the immediate dental care was not wrong. And while Ricardo would not have done it for a stranger, he certainly might have done the same thing for a friend. But the story of letting Luciano come and stay with him to ensure he made his dental appointment on time was just a ruse. Gregg wanted the lad in his apartment, and in his bed.

And Ricardo could understand why. Luciano was handsome, lean, with clear skin and nice, full lips. Ricardo himself had no taboos of any kind about sex. If Ricardo had happened to encounter Luciano in a gay bath house, for example, Ricardo would have put the moves on him as well. But consensual sex in a dark steam room where everyone leaves afterwards is different than moving a homeless stranger into your apartment in order to leverage them into sex. Ricardo agreed with Gregg's statement that Luciano was not gay, but Ricardo also thought that Luciano could be pressured into having sex simply to have free dental care and a bed to sleep in. And who knows what money Luciano might talk Gregg into giving him.

"Has he hit you up for money at all?" Ricardo asked.

"No, no, not at all," Gregg responded. "I've been paying for his meals of course, but he hasn't asked me for a dime."

"Okay. Well, just be careful."

"Oh, I will," Gregg said and smiled.

# Chapter 4:  Weeks Earlier

Morning comes early in Panama all year round. It was about six o'clock and the light was already strong even with the blinds drawn. Ricardo looked over at Alison. She was still asleep. He got up and brushed his teeth and then climbed back into bed, moved his naked body close to hers, and pulled the sheet and thin blanket aside to expose her naked torso. He stared at her body for a while. He loved the fact that she didn't shave her pubic hair. It was thick and curly and grew high on her lower stomach. She wouldn't wear tiny bikinis because the hair stuck out of the top. Ricardo gently stroked her thigh, then moved her leg slowly to one side, shifted his body down on the bed and over her, and started to lick her pussy. He could taste and smell the residue of last night's sex, which excited him more. Her pussy lips were closed and Ricardo pushed his tongue slowly in between them. The taste was tangy. So many men joke about women smelling fishy, but it just isn't true. Ricardo always found the smell and taste of a woman's pussy to be an important and wonderful aphrodisiac. He gently licked her clitoris.

"Oh... mmm... Ricardo? What are you...? No, I have to pee...."

"Too bad," Ricardo said, between licks. "You'll just have to hold it."

"Nooo... hmmm... I really have to pee..."

Her pussy lips were parted now and getting wet. "You taste so good, Alison." Ricardo said. She tried to sit up, but Ricardo reached up with his left arm and easily pushed her back down on the bed. She raised her knees. He pushed his tongue as deep as it would go into her vagina.

"Oh, Ricardo... mmmm... no..." she said and spread her legs apart. Ricardo continued to lick her pussy and run his fingers up and down her pussy lips. She lay there for a while, with her knees up and apart, moaning softly. Suddenly, she swung her right leg over his head, sat up, and hopped out of bed. "I really have to pee, and I want a shower." She started to walk into the bathroom.

"Okay," said Ricardo, "but you have to pee on me and then we'll both shower." He jumped out of bed, and grabbed her before she could sit on the toilet, and guided into the large shower stall, leaning her against the tile wall."

"Pee," he said.

"I can't," she complained, and started to pee. The pee hit Ricardo on the thigh. He laughed, caught some of the pee in his cupped hand and splashed it on his stomach. Then he reached up to her pussy and felt the force of the pee stream as it filled his cupped hand and spilled over.

"I think I have to pee too," he said. He straightened up, grabbed his cock for aim, and peed on Alison's leg. For a moment, the two pee streams collided and sprayed them both.

"God, you're such a pervert," she said.

"That's why you love me," he said, and kissed her.

Then he turned the water on and they both showered under the steamy water. One of the things that Ricardo liked about this apartment building was that it had the traditional large shower stall common in most Panamanian homes, but also had hot water tanks, which were not so common. There was plenty of room for Alison and Ricardo to shower together, to kiss, to lather up and rinse each other off, and kiss more.

Ricardo got out of the shower first and let Alison wash her hair, which he knew she took extra time for.

"I put a clean towel on the toilet seat for you," he said through the shower curtain as he was drying off.

After he was dry, he climbed back in bed and played with himself while he waited for her. By the time she got out and dried herself off, he was hard. As she walked over to the bed, he reached over to the bookshelf by the bed for the tube of lubricant.

# Chapter 5:   Paul

Gregg was right about one thing: Paul certainly kept to himself. Paul wouldn't even join the nightly drinking ritual at the patio picnic table, and that table was only twenty feet from his apartment door. Ricardo figured Paul to be in his late sixties, though it was hard to tell because he shaved his head and had no facial hair so there was no gray hair to measure his age. He had the kind of body that one could tell used to be quite athletic, but had gotten thick and out of shape. Gregg had mentioned that Dan, who lived in one of the upstairs apartments, had told him that Paul used to be a big-time surfer, before tearing up his knee. Gregg had also heard that there had been a knee operation that went wrong, and that had kept Paul from walking for almost a year, but that the malpractice lawsuit had funded his retirement. Several subsequent operations made it possible for Paul to walk again, but any type of sporting activity was now strictly forbidden. The one activity that Paul maintained from his glory surfing days was smoking marijuana. As far as Ricardo could tell, Paul spent every day, all day, sitting in his apartment, smoking marijuana and watching TV. If Ricardo sat outside on his tiny patio, he could hear Paul's TV playing next door. The apartment complex had cable, and while most of the shows were in Spanish, the system also carried ESPN in English, and Paul always had that channel on all day. Because Paul kept his door open for the breeze when he was home (as all the residents did, since there was no air conditioning), Ricardo could not only hear the TV when he sat outside, but he could smell the weed. Marijuana was, of course, illegal in Panama. But it was also routinely tolerated, especially if smoked by gringos. The gringo tourism money was too important to the Panamanian economy to let a little weed get in the way.

Ricardo didn't know where Paul got his marijuana. He assumed that Paul bought it off the local kids in the park, like most tourists did. During his first week at the Island of Misfits, Ricardo wondered why Ted (the live-in landlord and owner of the building) would allow such constant and obvious use of marijuana on his property. In the United States, such knowing acquiescence by a landlord would lead a gleeful district attorney to file a civil forfeiture action and take the building. But Panama had no such legal practice. Besides, Ricardo soon discovered that Ted would occasionally come down and smoke with Paul.

Ricardo also learned that Paul had lived at the Island for seven years and was considered one of the old-timers. Dan, who lived upstairs, had told Gregg that even though Paul could walk, he still had a lot of pain from the botched knee operation and was on a lot of pain medication. Other than noticing that Paul walked with a small limp, Ricardo couldn't confirm any of this with Paul, because Paul didn't talk to anyone except Ted. Ricardo would try and say hello to Paul if he saw him outside the apartment, and even tried to make small talk once when he saw him in the local grocery store, but Paul would have none of it. Paul simply nodded with a grimace and kept on moving.

Gregg had been right about another thing about Paul—that almost every weekend, Paul would drive to Panama City. Occasionally Ted went with him. While Dan owned a motorcycle, Paul was the only one in the apartment complex who had a car. Paul's use of his car gave credence to what Ricardo had heard about the bad knee, because he saw that Paul would drive even the two short blocks to the grocery store. Everyone else in the apartment complex would walk that distance.

Contrary to what Gregg had said about prostitutes, however, Ricardo never saw any women (or anyone else except Ted) visit Paul. Any visitors would have had to walk right by Ricardo's front window and open apartment door to get to Paul's apartment, and Ricardo would have seen them. However, Ricardo did assume that Paul's weekend trips to Panama City were for the purpose of visiting prostitutes, for two reasons: first, because there really wasn't any other reason to go to Panama City every weekend; and second, because one time Ricardo overheard Ted telling Dan (Ted's next door neighbor upstairs) what a good time he had had in Panama City the previous weekend when he had gone there with Paul. The tone of Ted's voice was the knowing tone that one man uses with another to imply that an especially good time was had.

Ricardo had mixed feelings about Paul. He gathered that at one time Paul had had a very successful surfing career, and Ricardo assumed that meant that Paul had enjoyed money and was accustomed to a bit of fame and probably a lot of female admirers. Losing money, fame, and female attention would turn any man bitter, especially if it was money, fame, and attention that one felt entitled to. So on one hand, Ricardo was sympathetic to Paul's plight. But on the other hand, Paul was so deep into his bitterness, so rebuffing of any friendly overtures, that it was hard to sustain any sympathy.

# Chapter 6:   Garden of Eden

"Do you think you'll stay here?" Alison had asked Ricardo during her visit.

"Mmmmm, you mean, here in Panama or here in this building?"

"Well, both. What are your plans?"

This was a couple of days after Alison had arrived at the Island of Misfits. She and Ricardo had finished an early dinner of fish, rice, and beans, and were having a beer outside at the picnic table under the palm tree. It was too early for the gaggle of regulars to gather at the table, so Ricardo had suggested they sit there and enjoy the first cool breezes of the late afternoon.

"Well, I certainly want to stay in Panama," Ricardo said. "I do have to go back to the states at least twice a year for various things. But my publisher is pretty good about cramming all my publicity crap to fit my schedule. I don't ever want to stop spending time in the States, but I really like living down here."

"It's been good for you. You're more relaxed down here than you were in the States."

"That's 'cause *you're* here, baby. Want another beer?"

"Not quite yet. What about this apartment? How long will you stay here?"

"I don't know," Ricardo responded. "These apartments are completely furnished, so it really is convenient. And so far, it's the only place in town that has internet. I mean, there are probably other houses with a room to rent with internet,

31

but I haven't found another furnished place that has the security, location, amenities and all the utilities included at this price. But on the other hand, it's full of gringos."

Alison laughed and quipped, "Said the gringo... How much do you pay?"

"It's about $250 a month, plus a couple of bucks if I want a housekeeper to come in and clean the apartment."

"Jesus," Alison said, "a housekeeper... you're so bourgeois. Your next book should be a travel book on Panama, called 'Bourgie on a Budget'."

Ricardo chuckled. "That's a good title, but yeah, no. I don't want to encourage more gringos to come down here. Really, all they do is ruin the place."

"But really, Ricardo, you could live this cheaply in the States. You know you could come and live with me in Santa Fe and pay me the $250 a month."

"And cook for you and take you out to dinner..."

"And have sex with me..."

Ricardo smiled sadly and said, "It's not the money. It's being away from everything... It's a place to write, to think, to not think... I can't describe it, but for all the problems Panama has—and it has *huge* problems—I really do love this place. Especially the people."

"And especially the women," Alison teased.

"None of them as good as you, baby."

"Liar," she responded. "You know, I've read your books, buddy. There's a lot of hookers in them... hookers and gay sex."

"I think if you check inside the very front page, just inside the cover, under the copyright, it clearly characterizes the book as fiction."

"Fiction my ass... my ass and probably several others."

"Well, you're the only one I love baby. I mean, in my own way."

"Jesus. I'll have that other beer now, please."

As Ricardo went inside to get more beer, he thought about the long road he had taken to get to Panama: how he had planned it for years, coming here every vacation, backpacking around, traveling by bus to explore all the towns, looking for somewhere where he could hide out and just write his books. That's what Panama is, he thought, just a place to hide out. And as far as hiding places go, this one was as good it was ever going to get, at least for him. He opened the refrigerator and grabbed two beers, popped them open, and headed back outside.

"Thanks," Alison said. "You know, I was thinking. What you really need is a two bedroom place. That way you'd have room for people to come and visit you. Your little studio here is kinda tiny."

"I know. It would be nice to have a bigger place. But there are only a few people I could tolerate as guests. If some couple wanted to come and see me, they would have to stay in some hotel in La Chorrera. This way, I have a great excuse for saying no—my place is too small. Besides, you're the only person I want to see."

Alison took a swig from her bottle then looked at Ricardo. You know," she said, "I envy you. You're living the dream. You're doing exactly what you want. That's the dream everyone has—to do exactly what they want."

Ricardo thought about that for a moment then said, "Well, it would be more accurate to say I'm doing what I can. It's not always a dream. But, yes, I'm lucky to be able to do this."

"It wasn't just luck, Ricardo. You made it happen."

"If it wasn't luck, Alison, I'm not sure what to call it. All of the other gringos in this complex made it here too. Would you say *they're* living the dream?"

"Maybe they are. Maybe they're living their dream."

"I don't know. Sometimes I think all we can do is do the best we can with the choices we are given."

"Speaking of choices, what are we going to do tomorrow?" Alison asked.

"Well, I was thinking we could catch a bus down to Playa Coronado. It's a little beach town about a forty-five-minute bus ride from here... got a nice beach. If you like it,

33

there's a little hotel there, and we could rent a room for the night and come back here the next day."

"Are there handsome surfer dudes there?" Alison asked with a smile.

"No... that's why I picked it."

# Chapter 7:  Dan

Dan was the youngest resident at the Island. Ricardo figured him for early fifties, maybe late forties. He was about five foot five, but built like a barrel—solid. It didn't surprise Ricardo to learn that Dan had been a police officer in Los Angeles for twenty years. According to Gregg, Dan had retired on a disability from the force and moved to Panama about three years ago. Gregg didn't know what the disability was. Dan did keep a motorcycle in the locked garage of the Island, and whatever the disability was or had been, it didn't keep Dan from riding his bike every day.

It was the motorcycle that had led to Ricardo and Dan's first conversation. Dan was in the garage area, taking the cover off his bike, when Ricardo happened to walk by and saw what the bike was.

"Whoa, dude," exclaimed Ricardo. "Is that a Virago?"

Dan smiled. "Sure is."

"Man, I loved those bikes! Is it a 750 or 1000?"

"750."

Ricardo stood there and admired the bike for a moment. Dan clearly kept it clean and in good repair. "What year is it?" he asked.

"1998."

"Wasn't that the year they stopped making them?" Ricardo asked.

"You know your Viragos. Yes, it was. I got the last one the dealer had." Dan said.

"By the way, I'm Ricardo. I moved in a couple of weeks ago."

"I'm Dan. I've seen you around."

They shook hands.

"How did you get it down here?" Ricardo asked, "and how do you get parts for it down here?"

"Parts are a problem. I've stockpiled a bunch of them over the years. I keep them in storage at a friend's bike shop in California. If I need something I can't get here, he ships it to me, but so far that's only happened twice in three years."

"And how did you get it down here?" Ricardo repeated.

"I shipped it. Cost me eight hundred, but it was worth it. I need my bike. Do you ride?"

Ricardo shook his head no. "It's been decades. About five years ago, I thought I might get one again, and so I took a motorcycle safety course to brush up. When I did that, I realized how much my reflexes had slowed down. To be honest, it kinda scared me."

"Yeah, I know what you mean," said Dan. "I don't take chances like I used to. Especially down here. People drive pretty wild down here."

"Yeah, I've noticed that."

Dan and Ricardo talked motorcycles for a few minutes more. Then, because Ricardo was aware that he had interrupted Dan's preparations for leaving, he said goodbye, but suggested they get together sometime for a beer.

Unlike most men's promises to get together for a beer sometime, this one actually happened. About a week later, Dan and Ricardo were sitting in a small cantina in Villa Rosario, drinking Balboa beers.

"I like this beer," Dan was saying. "It's got taste."

"Someone told me Balboa got bought out by Miller." Ricardo said.

"Well, not exactly," said Dan. "They got bought by SABMiller, which is a South African beer company that's been around since the 1800's. They eventually relocated to England. But SABMiller owns Miller in the U.S."

"Really? Shit, everything's global now, I guess."

The conversation eventually turned to how each of the two men had wound up in Panama. What Ricardo had heard about Dan being a former police officer in Los Angeles was true. He had been a detective in the Crenshaw District of LA. Mostly he investigated white-collar crime, but occasionally he got called into a drug or murder case when there were computer files that had to be analyzed. Ricardo shared how he had become a lawyer late in life, and had gone through a couple of stints of rehab for his drinking.

"I see the treatment was successful then," Dan said, pointing to Ricardo's second beer.

Ricardo smiled. "Well... I learned to live with it."

The two men spent an hour swapping war stories, Dan telling tales from the detective world and Ricardo telling stories from the legal world. Since Ricardo's legal field was probate, he was limited to recounting horror stories of what families did to each other to send the rich parent to an early grave, or cheat the other relatives out of an inheritance. Dan's stories were definitely better, and more interesting. The two men were getting along well and into several rounds of beer.

"Did you take early retirement, then?" asked Ricardo, not wanting to ask about disability directly. "I mean, you're kinda young for Social Security."

"Well, no," Dan said. "That is to say, yes and no. I got involved in a shooting incident during a police raid. It was a fairly big operation, organized crime shit, supposedly. I was only there to secure a bunch of computers that were supposed to be at this location. But the bad guys had somehow gotten tipped off, and there was a shoot-out. I ended up taking a bullet, even though I was standing way in the back of the crowd. It laid me low for awhile but it turned out not to be so bad. I was fine after about four months."

"But they gave you some kind of disability?"

"Well, I cut a deal with them."

Ricardo looked at Dan and just said, "Oh?"

"Well, it turned out that one of my friends was the

37

brother of one of the guys that we raided. They thought I had tipped him off, but I hadn't. They subpoenaed all my cell phone records and even confiscated my home computer. I found out later that they had kept me under surveillance for months after the raid. It was a bad scene. All those guys I thought were my friends. Anyway, they didn't find nothing, but I was persona non grata after that. Nobody wanted to partner with me. So my lawyer cut a deal with them. I applied for a disability pension, and they didn't contest it. Otherwise, I was going to sue them. But this way, I was outta their hair and it didn't cost them a lawsuit."

"Wow, Dan. I mean, I'm glad it worked out, but still, that really sucks."

"Yeah, I know. Twenty years down the toilet. Lost all my friends. But hey, you gotta roll with the punches. I'm down here, I got my bike. Life is good."

Ricardo decided to change the subject.

"So do you ride every day?" he asked.

"Uh huh. I have to. I ride to work."

This surprised Ricardo, given what Dan had just told him.

"Really?" he said, "where do you work?"

"At Berghoff's."

Ricardo had never heard of the place, and he must have had a puzzled look on his face, because Dan immediately added, "It's just outside of town."

"I'm not familiar with it," Ricardo said. "What is it?"

"It's a sportsbook place."

Ricardo was still confused. "What a sportsbook?" he asked.

Dan looked at him somewhat surprised. "It's for online gambling. You know, where people make bets online."

Ricardo had heard of online gambling of course, but thought that it was illegal.

"I thought the feds closed all those places down a few years back." Ricardo said.

"There were some high publicity raids and some indictments about two years ago, when all the places were concentrated in Costa Rica, but all that did was scatter the business. The owners just spread them out all over Central and South America and the Caribbean. And all the indictments were later quietly dropped. The business is bigger than ever."

"Really? How did you get into this line of work?"

"Well, my buddy, the one whose brother got busted, he felt so bad for me getting railroaded by my own department that he helped set me up down here. I mean, the disability pension check is nice, it's good, and it more than covers all the basics, but the extra money I make down here is pure gravy. I can go to Panama City on the weekends and party like there's no tomorrow."

"What about the local cops, here in Villa Rosario? They don't hassle the business?" Ricardo asked.

"Hell, no!" Dan laughed. "I know them all well, especially the chief José Fernando. We even talk shop occasionally. You know, investigative techniques and shit."

Ricardo pondered all this information for a minute and then pressed on. "You know, if you don't mind my saying so, Dan, that seems like an odd profession for an ex-detective to get into. I mean, aren't you walking right up to some legal line?"

"Well, no. I mean, it's true that the laws keep changing, but Berghoff's has lawyers that track everything. The legal issues all depend on how you process the bets and whether or not you advertise. Besides, it's almost impossible for the U.S. to complain about foreign online gambling when anyone in the States can go online and bet the horses all day long. The international courts keep pointing that out to the U.S. government."

Ricardo thought about this for a moment. He had been to the race tracks in New York and it was true. There were more terminals set up to make online bets on other horse races in other states than there were betting windows to make bets on the actual race going on that minute at the track.

"Yeah, I can see that, Dan. But I meant it more as a

39

philosophical question. It just seems like a one-eighty from what you were doing."

Dan pursed his lips. "Well, just like you said, I realized that I could learn to live with it. My head kind of got turned around when the department fucked me over. Everything I had was gone, and I had to learn how to think differently. I learned more about the law and life those few months when I was in the hospital than I had ever learned on the force."

"Well, Dan," said Ricardo raising his glass, "as Charles Darwin once said, here's to adaptability."

"Ha! I'll drink to that," Dan said.

# Chapter 8:   Besos

Alison and Ricardo were lying in bed, kissing. They had spent the day on the beach at Playa Coronado, swimming, sunbathing, playing frisbee, walking, sampling ceviche from the local food stands, looking for shells and pebbles, and—despite liberal amounts of sunscreen—getting sunburned.

After some fish tacos and beer at one of the beachside stands, they retired to their hotel room, took a cool shower to ease the sunburn, rubbed each other with lotion, and slipped under the sheets. The sunburn put a damper on making love, but it didn't stop them from cuddling and kissing.

"You're hot," Alison said.
"Hmmm, thank you baby."
"No, I mean temperature. I can feel the heat coming off your skin."
"Yeah, you too. Kiss me some more."

Ricardo loved kissing and he especially loved kissing Alison. She had full soft lips, and she would playfully use her tongue and dart in and out of Ricardo's mouth, and then trace the outline of his lips with the tip of her tongue.

Ricardo thought kissing was the best part of making love. With sex, there's always some drive to build it up, increase the pleasure, raise the tension, work towards orgasm... but with kissing, it was just kissing. Every kiss was its own little pleasure. There was nothing to increase, no goal to get to, just an endless variety of how two lips can touch. And especially in moments like this evening, when it was understood that they were not going to make love (well, probably not, but when there was an unspoken understanding that the kissing could go on for hours) there was just a quiet pure joy of intimacy.

"You know, I love you, Alison," he said between kisses.
"I love you too, Ricardo."
She pulled him closer to her and kissed him harder, then said, "Then why don't you come to Santa Fe this summer?"
"Hmmm, too hot."
Well, how 'bout this November?
"Too cold."
"You bum," she said, and kissed him again.

Ricardo pulled his head back, and looked at her. She was beautiful, and he did love her, but he knew the limitations that each of their lives had.
"You know, Alison, our love works because of our art, not because of our... our personalities. I don't know the right word. But the fact that you hole up in Santa Fe and paint for months on end—those beautiful paintings—and I hole up here and write, and then... we're like two depleted batteries, we need to recharge ourselves, and so we hook up for the pure energy... but we do it for our art, or because of our art, because you know how it is, we always go back to our art. Remember when you were in Africa painting those elephant bone pictures and I came to stay for a month, and you kicked me out because you said I was in your way? Kicked me out in Africa! But you were right to do so. Those pictures needed to be painted. Whatever happened to them by the way?"
"Sold them this year."
"Really? Good money?"
"It'll cover the rent for the next two years."
"Good girl. Here, kiss me again."
They kissed some more. Then Ricardo asked, "Did you sell all of them?"

"All of what?"

"The elephant bone paintings."

"Uh huh. Some gallery in Chicago took a lot of them, and then a gallery in Hawaii took a couple, and the rest went to private buyers," she said.

"Mmmm, I really liked those paintings."

"Well, I've got some new paintings now I think you'd like. I'm doing a show in Santa Fe in December. You ought to come up and see them."

"Hmmmpf," he said. "Too cold... but I *would* like to see them. You are such a good artist. What was I saying about art? Oh, yeah. Every time we try and spend more than two weeks together, it interferes with our art, and we each start to get antsy."

"God, you are such a bullshitter, don Ricardo." And she started kissing him again.

They lay there kissing for another fifteen minutes or so. Ricardo started to explore the roof of Alison's mouth and the feel of her teeth with his tongue. Alison made him stick his tongue out and sucked on it. Then he turned her head and ran his tongue all inside her ear. They kissed lightly and they kissed hard, wrapped in each other's arms.

"Did you get sunburned all over?" Alison asked.

"Pretty much."

She reached down and felt his cock. "Here, too?"

"Well, no."

She eased down under the sheets and took his cock into her mouth and began to work it, holding and gently squeezing his balls.

"Oh, sweet Jesus," Ricardo said before exhaling. "I'm the luckiest man alive."

# Chapter 9:   Ted

Ted owned the apartment complex, and he lived in the second floor corner studio that had the best view overlooking Villa Rosario and the valley beyond. He did everything himself concerning the apartment: interviewing prospective tenants, collecting the rent, doing any necessary repairs, everything except the yard maintenance which he farmed out to some local laborers. But even then, he would stand there and keep a close eye on them. Ricardo had the impression that he was retired ex-military, because he liked everything super-orderly and run right. Ricardo liked that about Ted—he was a good landlord. If something needed fixing, it got fixed right away. But Ricardo didn't know Ted well, and in fact, never got to know him well. Ted kept all his relationships with the tenants on a strictly non-personal basis, except for his obvious friendship with Paul downstairs, and a somewhat friendly relationship with Dan. Because Dan lived in the apartment next to Ted, they had more opportunity to chat. Most of what Ricardo knew about Ted came from Dan.

Dan had told Ricardo that Ted bought the building fourteen years ago. Dan didn't know if Ted was former military or not, but knew that he had obtained permanent residency status in Panama by marrying a Panamanian woman years ago. But they didn't live together. Dan claimed that Ted had mentioned once that he and his wife owned a house together somewhere outside of town, and Dan had even met Ted's wife one time. But clearly Ted lived full-time at the Island of Misfits. His apartment had the interior look of someone who had lived there a long time. There was shelving unlike the other apartments, and file cabinets, and artwork on the walls. The way Dan described the inside of Ted's apartment gave Ricardo the same impression as Ted's behavior—everything was clean and orderly.

Ricardo wondered if Ted's marriage was one of convenience, some type of legal maneuver that was necessary in order to buy the apartment building. Ricardo had heard a rumor that foreigners weren't allowed to own more than 49% of any property in Panama. Dan didn't know. Dan said that the few times that he had heard Ted talk about his wife, it was in positive terms. On the other hand, Dan claimed that Ted was clearly in a sexual relationship with Alma, the cleaning woman who came to the apartment complex once a week to do laundry and clean the apartments. Such cleaning services were not included in the rent. Tenants had to request them from Ted each week. Most of the tenants washed their own clothes—there was a small "lavaropa" sink in the back of each studio apartment designed for hand-washing small amounts of clothes, plus a line above the sink for hang-drying. But for a few dollars, Alma would change the sheets and towels, clean the apartment, and mop the floors. Some of the older residents had Alma do this on a weekly basis. The others would only request it as needed. Dan told Ricardo that every Wednesday, Alma would come over in the mornings and clean whichever apartments needed cleaning. She would bag any dirty sheets and towels to take home with her to wash and bring back the following week. According to Dan, every Wednesday after she was done cleaning, he could hear her taking a shower in Ted's apartment. Then he could hear them making love in Ted's bed. Then he would hear Alma take another shower, and then she would leave. Dan claimed the routine never varied. He didn't know if Alma was married or just liked to be clean. And of course, he never asked Ted.

Ricardo accepted Dan's description of Ted's affair as true, and he also believed that Ted occasionally went with Paul to Panama City to visit prostitutes. From these pieces of information, Ricardo assumed that Ted's marriage to his wife was in name only. Ricardo didn't have any opinion one way or the other about marriages of convenience. Over the years, he had had many gay friends who were in sexless marriages that they described as both loving and convenient. Of course, Ricardo didn't know if either one of those labels was really true. If it's one area that people lie the most about, it's their marriages. But it was of no concern to Ricardo.

However, one thing that Dan told Ricardo did bother him—Dan had overheard Paul complaining to Ted about Gregg and Luciano, and he heard Paul refer to Gregg as *that dirty little fag*.

# Chapter 10: Alejandro

Alejandro was not a resident of the Island, but he knew most of the residents because he managed the grocery store two blocks away. Alejandro was gay and was a friend of Miguel. Miguel was the co-owner of Los Cuñados, one of Ricardo's favorite restaurants in La Chorrera. Miguel had introduced Alejandro to Ricardo several months before Ricardo had moved to Villa Rosario. In fact, it was Alejandro who had told Ricardo about the Island apartments and had told Ricardo that Ted had a vacancy there.

Alejandro had deep connections in the community of Villa Rosario. The fact that he was flamboyantly gay did not bother anyone in the town, and perhaps it even made it easier for him to get to know people, because they loved to gossip with him. Plus, his position at the town's main grocery store kept him in daily contact with people. Ricardo didn't know that, of course, when he first met him months earlier at Miguel's restaurant. He just thought that Alejandro was an attractive and animated gay man. The two became friends. After Ricardo moved to the Island, he and Alejandro began getting together once a week for dinner. Ricardo soon discovered that Alejandro was a reliable source of information about everything and everyone in the town. It was over dinner one night, about a month after Alison had left, that the subject of Gregg and Luciano came up.

"Oh, that Gregg," Alejandro was saying. "He hits on everything in pants. He has that—what do you gringos call it? Gaydar? The first time he came into my store, he spotted me and made a beeline straight to the counter. I was helping people pay their electric bills. And he tried to *cut* in front of them! I knew what he was up to, of course. But I had to put on my official voice for the other customers and say 'I'll be with you in a minute, sir.' The locals liked that—make the gringo wait his turn. When it was his turn, he introduced himself to me as if we were old friends and asked me out right on the spot. But no, definitely not my type."

"That's funny," Ricardo said. "But I can so see him doing that."

"Oh he's always on the hunt. Nice enough, friendly, educated... but on the hunt. I don't like that type. Me, I'm very particular about who I sleep with. I don't sleep with just anyone, even if they're cute. I have to like them. Gregg, I think, would sleep with anyone. I asked him one time what kind of men he likes, and he said, 'men I haven't had sex with yet'. Can you imagine that? No, not my type. But persistent. I did have lunch with him just one time because he was so persistent, and the conversation was very pleasant, but afterwards, of course, he asked me to come over to his apartment. I had to set him straight. I am no whore."

"I know what you mean," Ricardo said. "Have you seen his latest companion?"

"Oh, that Luciano boy!? I know him. He's no good. Homeless. Always into trouble. He hangs around that park in La Chorrera where gay men cruise."

"That's where Gregg said he met him—in some park in La Chorrera, but Gregg said he wasn't gay."

"No, he's not," Alejandro said. "But he's poor and lazy. So he lets men blow him if they give him money."

"Really? Gregg told me he hasn't given him any money," Ricardo said.

"I don't think he has, but he hasn't needed to yet. He paid for all of the boy's dental work—the wisdom tooth, the fillings, the prescriptions, all of his meals. And he's letting him sleep in his apartment, and it's been maybe three weeks since the dentist visit that he's been living there, and so he lets Gregg blow him."

"Really? Gregg told you that?" Ricardo asked.

"No, Luciano did! I asked him directly and he told me. People cannot lie to me—I am too handsome."

Ricardo laughed. "What else did he tell you?"

"Well, he won't let Gregg fuck him—he's no fool. And he won't blow Gregg, but he'll let Gregg blow him and then Gregg will jack off. Luciano's got a good deal—free rent, a nice bed, all his meals... He won't ask Gregg for money until Gregg gets ready to return to the States. Right now, Luciano's got a good sugar daddy. He doesn't want to fuck that up."

Ricardo shook his head. "That's so sad. I mean, I know they're both adults. And I know that they're both just using each other, and people get into relationships all the time where they use each other and so I don't want to judge it, but...."

"Oh, I'll judge it!" Alejandro interrupted. "I don't like that boy, and I don't like what he's up to. I don't like it when people use someone else. I don't care that Gregg wants it. And I don't even like Gregg that much. But I *definitely* do not like what Luciano's doing. He's just using Gregg. And Gregg's using him. Even that time when I had lunch with Gregg, he tried to buy my lunch. I said no. He was so persistent. He kept saying, 'oh it's an American custom. I make so much more money than you; let me just pay for this one meal.' But I told him no. I don't use anyone. I pay my own way. I don't take free meals from anyone except family. People like Gregg and Luciano, they think money is everything. It's not. It just gets them into trouble."

52

# Chapter 11: Alison

It was toward the end of Alison's two-week visit when she and Ricardo had their usual spat about commitment. Alison had been asking Ricardo again to visit her in Santa Fe and it got on Ricardo's nerves.

"You know, a couple of days ago you said you might come up in December," she said.

"I did?"

"God, you never remember anything! I'm doing that show in December, remember? New paintings? You said you would come up to see them."

"Oh, yeah. When's that show?"

"It's the first full week in December. I don't remember the exact dates. Starts on a Tuesday and runs eight days."

"Well, I don't know. I don't know what my publisher has lined up for me. I'll have to check with him."

"Why do you always have to coordinate everything with your publisher? Why can't you just come up for a visit?"

"Well, I don't want to commit to visiting you if he's got me signing books in some other city."

"You always use that excuse but you never come and see me. I always have to come and visit *you*."

"I went to Africa, Remember?"

"That was four fucking years ago, Ricardo! And it was only because you had to be in Europe anyway. And I had to plead with you for that visit."

"Well, I have to coordinate with my publisher, Alison. I have commitments!"

"No, that's the problem, you don't have commitments. You just use that as an excuse to avoid commitments. You

53

let me into your life for a few weeks and then you shut me out for months! And then six months after that, I read some description in your book and I know it's about me!"

Ricardo was exasperated now. He hated fighting. He hated the tightening it caused in his chest. He hated having to defend himself. He started to raise his voice.

"What's that got to do with anything?" he started, but then stopped short. He closed his eyes and took a deep breath.

"What are we fighting about, Alison? Is it about your show in December? Or are we fighting about something else?"

"We're fighting about the fact that I hate how you want to control our relationship."

Ricardo took another deep breath. He had been down this road with Alison before, and he didn't want to go any further.

"To the extent that I do that, it's because I don't know any other way. I love you, Alison. I love being with you. But I can't be with you, or anyone, for long periods of time... I just can't do it. The fact that you may be right about me not committing doesn't change it. I know my limitations, baby. We've had this fight before. You know I love you, and you know I would do anything for you."

"Then will you come up for the show?"

Ricardo paused. He was trapped now. He knew he was right, that he couldn't spend extended periods of time with anyone; he had never been able to do that. But he also knew that Alison was right about one thing: his inability to commit to a relationship left him isolated... in control, but isolated. He just didn't like her fighting style. He found it manipulative. But he also knew that his style—keeping her at a distance much of the time—was equally manipulative.

"Okay. One week. You know I hate Santa Fe in the winter, but I'll come for you. One week. Email me the dates when you get home and I'll tell my publisher not to schedule anything for me then."

"Oh, I know you, señor Ricardo. You'll tell your

publisher to schedule something right after that week so you'll have an excuse to leave."

"And if I did that Alison, would that be so wrong? If I come and see you like I'm promising, what does it matter if I do some publicity afterwards? Writing is my art, and I have to publicize it, just like you have to organize shows to sell your paintings. And by the way, I just remembered, that last show of yours in Chicago I came to last year—"

"*Two* years ago," she interrupted.

"Okay, two years ago. There were a bunch of dinner parties with local press and articles about me being there at your show. Are there going to be more of those?"

"Well, yeah, there might be..."

"Uh huh."

"Well," she said, imitating Ricardo, "painting is my art, and I have to publicize it."

Ricardo gave a small laugh. "Okay, baby. Truce, then? I'll come for a week in December."

"Truce," she said.

# Chapter 12: Jonathan

If Gregg was the Island's gay expat predator, Ricardo decided, then Jonathan was the Island's straight "sexpat". He lived upstairs, next to Dan. When he was in town, he drank every night at the table under the palm tree on the patio with the usual crowd and talked openly about his sexploits.

"I love this country," Jonathan would say, starting another story about some local girl. "I spent last weekend on the beach at Bocas del Toro... beautiful women there. Let me tell you, the women here just have a different attitude about sex. I met this little Panamanian chick, about twenty years old, dark and slim, sitting on the beach, and I just flat asked her to come back to my hotel. She said, 'I am not that easy'. and I said 'well, I've got a hundred bucks that says otherwise'. Ha! she was great. Rode me like a Texas cowgirl. Love this country!"

Ricardo soon discovered that Gregg hated Jonathan. "He's so boorish," Gregg told Ricardo. "He's always bragging about some girl he banged. He's just so full of shit! He's one of the reasons I don't drink out there with those guys. I can't stand his stories."

Ricardo didn't comment on that—he had his own opinion about why Gregg didn't drink with the other men. He did agree that Jonathan's stories got old real fast, but he thought they were probably true. In just the few months that Ricardo had lived at the Island, he had seen Jonathan bring a number of young women up to his apartment. The first time Ricardo saw this, he was sitting inside Dan's apartment having a beer with Dan. The apartment door was open as usual for the breeze, when Jonathan walked by, escorting a woman towards his apartment next door. Jonathan made it a point to say hello to Ricardo and Dan, just to point out that he had a woman.

"Hello, gentlemen," he said as he walked by. "Can't stop and talk now."

After they heard Jonathan's apartment door close, Dan said, "I recognize her. She's a barfly down at that cantina next to the park downtown. Not bright enough to be a hooker, but trying to be. Most of the time she just hits you up for free drinks, but at the end of each month she needs to get the rent money together so she'll turn a trick or two."

"Really?" Ricardo said. "Has Jonathan brought her here before?"

"I don't know. I haven't seen her with him before, but he brings so many different ones up here. Claims he likes variety. He's got a whole routine down."

"What do you mean?" Ricardo asked.

"Well, by now he's poured her a drink, and in a minute, you'll hear the music go on. And in about five minutes you'll hear him pounding her on the bed. His bed is up against this wall here," Dan said, pointing at the wall. "And he just bangs away. So I hear it all. I think he's somewhat of an exhibitionist. He wants everyone to know he's fucking. I'm surprised he even closes his door."

Just then, Ricardo heard music come on next door.

"See? What did I tell you?" Dan said.

"So, you get to hear Ted on one side and Jonathan on the other?" Ricardo asked.

"Ah, Ted's okay. He and Alma are pretty quiet. But Jonathan's loud."

"How often does Jonathan bring someone up?" Ricardo asked.

"About once a week when he's in town, but he's only here about two weeks out of the month. He splits his time between here and the Dominican Republic. He spends a lot of time at that Sosua beach town there. That place is just a sex town. Nothing but hookers. I think he only stays here to rest up."

"He must have money," Ricardo said.

"He must. I don't talk to him that much. He's more friends with the nightly drinking group, especially Carl. Carl hangs on every word, and Jonathan needs an audience. He keeps promising to take Carl to Sosua with him."

"I can't keep everyone straight," said Ricardo. "Is Carl the short balding guy? Kinda not too bright?"

"That's him," Dan said. "Came down here about a month before you did. Totally lost. Retired from some factory job in Ohio. He read somewhere that Panama was the place to retire to, so he sold everything and moved down here. But he didn't have a plan. Can't speak Spanish. He's got nothing to do down here. I think that's why he's latched on to Jonathan. When Jonathan is gone, Carl just sits around like some sad puppy waiting for him to return. You watch, he's starting to talk like Jonathan now."

"I really don't talk to him," Ricardo said. "Not sure why. He just doesn't seem that interesting."

"He's not. And you may not get a chance to talk with him. I'll bet he won't make it here another two months. He'll slink back to Ohio with his tail between his legs."

"Even if Jonathan takes him to Sosua?"

"Jonathan's not going to pay his way, and Carl can't afford to go. Besides Jonathan needs an audience, not a witness. Makes for better stories."

Just then the banging next door started.

"Jesus, that's loud," Ricardo said.

"Yup, sit back and wait. In a few more minutes he'll start bellowing like a bull."

# Chapter 13:   Ladies' Night

Of course, Ricardo himself was no stranger to prostitutes. He had written about them extensively in his books, and his writings were often based on his own experiences. He didn't hold the usual judgments about prostitution. He believed that most women prostituted themselves at one point or another—that is, traded sex for material advantages. It was just a question of degree, of where someone fell on the spectrum. He had met too many women who had admitted they married for money, and then later admitted they divorced for more money. Men, of course, were the same. Actually, more so, just in reverse. They traded lifestyle or material things for sex. But it was the exact same type of transaction, the same type of trade.

Alison was one of the few people with whom he could talk about this issue. During her beginning days as an artist, before she was making a living with her paintings, and before she knew Ricardo, she had gone on several Craigslist dates for money. She was actually proud of the fact that she made four hundred dollars on one of her dates. She *did* say it was worth every penny, because she didn't like the guy at all.

She had told Ricardo about it one night, years ago, back in the States, when they were lying in bed talking about sex and prostitution. Ricardo had just finished telling her a long story about a prostitute named Haley, who he used to see on a regular basis, how he felt he might have been in love with her, and how the relationship worked great so long as they stayed in the brothel. But when they tried to take their relationship outside of the brothel, things fell apart.

That's when Alison told him the story of her Craigslist days. Ricardo said he understood, and then they both talked about the ethics of prostitution. Ricardo was trying to explain his theory that everyone, in one way or another, at one time or another, sells themselves.

"It's kinda like this old story George Burns used to tell," Ricardo said.

"Who?" Alison asked.

"An old comedian, before your time. Anyway, he said he was doing a show in Las Vegas and he gets into an elevator and there's this beautiful woman there, and they're riding up in the elevator together, just the two of them. And he turns to her and says, 'Will you sleep with me if I buy you a mink coat?' And she says, very coyly, 'Maybe.' And then, he says 'Will you do it for twenty dollars?' And the woman gets all offended and says, 'What do you think I am—a whore?!' And George Burns says, 'Well, we've already established that. Now we're just haggling over price.'"

"Ha! That's funny," Alison said. "And true as far as it goes, but, you know, there's a million different sides to that question."

"Of course... but say more," Ricardo said.

"Well, the woman who introduced me to the Craigslist idea, her name was Amanda, she was this other artist I knew. Not great, but she had potential. She was painting during the day and selling 'dates' on Craigslist at night, you know, to make ends meet. And she was making good money, and I was broke. So she showed me how to post an ad, how to arrange to meet the guy in a public place to check him out, how to negotiate price, all that shit."

"Okay..."

"I did it a couple of times. But then, I sold some paintings and got a little money, so I didn't have to do it anymore. But Amanda kept doing it, because the money was too good to pass up. Then, she starting doing dates during the day out of her apartment, and then she started working for an escort service full time. Stopped doing her art altogether. Then I heard that she was doing a fair amount of drugs, because that work can get to you, you know. And then, about a year later, I learned she had overdosed and died. The coroner listed it as accidental, but one of her close friends told me she thought it was suicide."

"Sad," Ricardo said.

"But my point is, Ricardo, that while I agree with you, that everyone sells a bit of themselves from time to time, real prostitution can warp a person. I mean, can you imagine having to fuck nine or ten women a day?"

"Well, Alison, that would be a physical impossibility. My dick would fall off."

"Okay, fine. Then, imagine you had to let nine or ten guys fuck your ass every day... or you had to blow them every day, and you didn't feel sexy about most of them."

"Okay, hold on," Ricardo said. "I'm closing my eyes... okay, sucking off ten guys... is this all at once? like a bukkake session? Wait, wait... I'm getting excited...."

"Stop it! I'm serious. Imagine you worked at a brothel and had no choice. And these guys come in one after the other, ugly guys, old guys, fat guys, guys with bad breath, guys covered in body hair, guys who might have AIDS, and you had to let each one fuck you."

"Well, okay, Alison. I've heard that argument before, but all the prostitutes I've known have been independent. They chose their hours, they chose the men, they chose the number of partners they had in a day or week. Some of them only saw a few regulars each week."

"That's probably true, Ricardo. But you operate at a higher level of prostitution. I guarantee you that the vast majority of prostitutes work in those brothels where they don't have a choice. They're not pretty enough or not smart enough to do any better. But they need the money."

"Okay. I concede that's probably true," Ricardo said. "But the fact that some people get exploited doesn't mean that the concept of prostitution is wrong. I mean, the fact that the best job a particular person can get is as a dishwasher doesn't mean that the concept of restaurants is wrong, or the fact that most marriages fail doesn't make the concept of marriage wrong. Wait a minute... strike that, I don't want to talk about marriage."

"Don't get so defensive Ricardo," Alison laughed. "I'm basically agreeing with you. I'm not saying prostitution is wrong. Hell, I did it myself! But *I am* saying that prostitution is not the elevated liberated occupation you paint it to be in your books. It's a slippery slope, like everything else in life. And on any slippery slope, the vast majority of people slide all the way to the bottom."

"I did read an article in Cosmo once that said that said that if women acted more like prostitutes in bed with their husbands, they could keep their marriage together," Ricardo said.

"What, charge them by the hour?"

"No, dress up and act sexy. That's what it is, you know, Alison. It's the illusion. The garter belts and the bustiers, and the little whips."

"Oh, so you're saying I'm not good enough for you?" Alison teased.

"No, baby, you're perfect. I'm talking about married people. You know... *them*."

"Oh, yeah... *them*."

Ricardo was quiet for a minute. Then he said, "You know, I knew this guy once years ago in New York. Rich guy. Financed a lot of Hollywood movies, I mean, he would just invest in them, but they would credit him as a 'producer'. His business card even said 'movie producer' but he really didn't know shit about good movies. But he was good at picking popular movies to invest in, or maybe just lucky. Anyway, so, he had this reputation as movie producer. I met him at some party, and he took a liking to me. This was years ago when I was way more handsome. Anyway, this guy was bisexual, and he loved swinger parties and orgies and the like, And at the time, he had this young starlet... She couldn't have been more than eighteen or nineteen, and he was in his mid to late forties, and he was always going on about her to everyone, about how he was going to make her a star in some upcoming movie... and of course, he was feeding her this line too, and fucking her night and day. So, one time, before I ever met her, he shows me her picture... some publicity shots he had done. And I'm looking at her, and I'm trying to be nice because he's standing there beaming as he shows me these half naked pictures of this girl. And *she did* have a great body, but she just wasn't star material. I mean, she wasn't pretty or intriguing or anything. She was just an average eighteen-or nineteen-year-old girl. Anyway, there's a point here..."

"I hope so," Alison laughed.

"Oh yeah, so he was using her to have these three-way sex scenes with men. He claimed she loved them. And he invited me to one."

"Oh, really?" Alison sat up in bed. "And did you go?"

"Of course. And I met her, and she wasn't very personable, but hell, she could have been stoned. But the three of us had sex."

"Really? And how was that?" Alison asked.

"Well, I liked it. But the point is, really this is all to your point, is that she wasn't really into it. I mean, she was there, she was participating. But...she was, like, distracted the whole time. Later, when I thought about it, I decided that she was playing the part of being his sexy girlfriend so that she could get that Hollywood role he kept promising her."

"And did she?"

"Of course not. I ran into him about six months later, and asked him about her. and he was so flippant. 'Oh her,' he said, 'Well, that didn't work out. I don't know where she is now.' I mean, he was just using her, but she was using him too, hoping to be a star."

"Hmm," Alison said. "She had something in common with that Amanda girl."

"Yeah, well, I think keeping both body and soul intact is simply hard work. It has nothing to do with the occupation of prostitution. Maybe it's life that is the slippery slope." Ricardo said.

"Well if I had a drink, I'd drink to that," Alison said.

"Oh, did you want a drink?" Ricardo asked.

"No, too early, come here and let's cuddle."

*    *    *

That particular conversation happened years ago, long before Alison's recent visit to the Island of Misfits. But now it has been several weeks since her departure, and tonight, Ricardo was in La Chorrera, sitting at the small bar located in the back the Los Cuñados restaurant, remembering that long-ago conversation with Alison, and missing her. He was thinking of all the conversations he had had with her over the years, and how easy it was to talk with her. They kept in contact via email and Skype, of course, but it wasn't the same as having her with him. He missed lying next to her and talking, and he missed her touch.

This was the first night since she had flown back to the States that he had ventured out in search of female company. He came to Los Cuñados not only because it was his favorite restaurant, but because he needed somewhere to think about exactly what he wanted to do. He had had a nice dinner and then had moved over to the bar.

Miguel, one of the two brothers-in-law who owned the restaurant, came up to him at the bar. Miguel was Ricardo's oldest friend in Panama. They had met two years ago at one of La Chorrera's bathhouses. Miguel was married and was, like many Panamanians, deep in the closet. But he and Ricardo were able to speak candidly.

"How are you doing, my friend?" Miguel asked, "How was your dinner?"

"Dinner was marvelous as always, Miguel. But I'm at loose ends tonight."

"Oh," said Miguel, in a low voice. "Thinking about heading over to the bathhouse?"

"No... I don't know, I was actually thinking about heading over to Jenny's," Ricardo said. Jenny's was a brothel that Ricardo had been to a number of times and liked.

"Ah, yes. That place," said Miguel. "Well, it is Thursday."

"Yeah? So?"

"Well," Miguel said, "I understand Thursday night is ladies' night there."

"Really? What does that mean?"

"It doesn't mean anything," Miguel laughed, "it's just a little joke of mine."

Ricardo smiled. "Actually, that is kinda funny."

"You know," Miguel said, "she comes in here to eat fairly often with her husband."

"Who does?" asked Ricardo.

"Jenny," said Miguel.

"She's married?" exclaimed Ricardo. "Really?"

"Oh yes. Very nice husband. Plus, she has two grown kids. Luckily, both of them are boys."

"Really?... Married? I can't quite visualize that," said Ricardo. He sat there a moment and thought about that. Jenny was about fifty-two years old, short, what might be described as matronly-looking. But she always dressed well, and the brothel she ran in La Chorrera was small but elegant. She was very particular about who she let work there, and never had more than four or five girls working for her at any one time. But they were the best local girls that La Chorrera had to offer. Jenny would only employ Panamanian women. Some of the other brothels let Colombians work in their establishments, because some of the Colombian women were stunning, but Jenny refused to let Colombians work in her brothel. "They are all thieves," she told Ricardo one time. "You cannot trust them." Ricardo liked her place because it was safe, and there was no pressure. He could come in, have a cup of coffee (Jenny refused to serve alcohol) and chat with Jenny before heading upstairs with one of the girls. Plus, he liked that each room had its own shower and clean towels. It was a good operation.

"Wow, I guess it's hard for me to think of her outside of the brothel," Ricardo said.

"Everyone has to eat," laughed Miguel.

"No," said Ricardo, "I can see her eating here. What I mean is, it's hard for me to think of hookers or madams leading normal lives, going shopping, things like that... Well, no, that's not it... it's that right before you walked up, I was sitting here remembering a conversation Alison and I once had..."

"Ah," said Miguel, "your little artist friend. You talk about her a lot. You should marry her."

"Yeah, no, Miguel. But thanks for the thought. Anyway, I was just remembering this conversation I had with her about prostitutes. She was basically saying that I don't really understand them, even though I think I do."

Miguel sat down beside Ricardo and said, in a serious tone of voice, "Ah my friend, she is right. No man ever understands a woman prostitute. It is not just the world's oldest profession; it is the world's most mysterious profession. Male prostitutes are different—they are just angry, they start off angry and get worse, but women prostitutes are a whole other world. It is like the profession is a potion, a magical potion that they drink, and it changes them..."

"Yeah, that's what Alison was saying... that the profession hardens them," Ricardo said.

"No, I would not agree... I think each one is different... the potion they drink changes each of them, and they don't know how they will turn out. Maybe they are courageous to drink it, or maybe foolish, I don't know. But it transforms them. Some become worse, but some become better. Some become rich, and others poor. Take Jenny, for example. Years ago, she was just another single mom with no skills, living in Panama City, trying to support two babies by cleaning houses. She started selling herself to make money, and she was good at it. But she didn't like how the brothels were run. So she saved her money, worked very hard, made her kids go to school, and when she got too old to turn tricks, she bought that little house here in La Chorrera. And today, she runs it better than any brothel in Panama City. Along the way, she found a good husband. They come to my church on Sundays."

"No kidding," said Ricardo. "And people don't gossip?"

"No, she does a lot of work with the church. She is

well-liked. The men, of course, all pretend that they don't know her. And their wives all choose to believe that. Church is a wonderful place to watch the drama of life." Miguel laughed.

"Wow," said Ricardo. "I don't know if I can look at her the same way now."

"Well, I guess you'll have to go to the bathhouse now," said Miguel slyly.

"No, shit… I don't know, Miguel. I'm just at such loose ends. I was intending to go to Jenny's but now, I don't know."

"I think you miss your *novia*." Miguel said, using the Spanish word for fiancée.

"She's not my novia; she's my *amante*," said Ricardo.

"Okay, my friend. Whatever you say. But I think you miss her."

"Fuck you, but yeah, I do," Ricardo admitted.

"When is she coming back?" asked Miguel.

"I don't know. But I'm going to go visit her in December," said Ricardo.

"So, you have plenty of time."

"Yeah, I do… that's one thing I've got, is time."

"May I make a suggestion, my friend?"

"Of course, Miguel."

"Go to Jenny's tonight. Then, this Saturday, go to the bathhouse. If you are still missing your little artist friend come next Monday, then she is your *novia*, and not an *amante*."

With that, Miguel got up, said his goodbyes and went to check on his other guests. Ricardo sat there for a while, sipping his wine, just thinking. He decided to take Miguel's advice, but not tonight. Tonight, he decided he just wasn't in the mood. He would catch the bus back to Villa Rosario. But he decided that, next week, he would come back to La Chorrera and go to Jenny's, no matter what mood he was in.

70

# Chapter 14: Luciano

"When do you go back to the States?" Ricardo asked Gregg. Ricardo had joined Gregg for a morning coffee at the table beneath the palm tree on the patio.

"In about two weeks," Gregg said. "My visa is up, and I've got some legal stuff there I have to deal with."

"Is Luciano still here?"

"Yeah, he's sleeping right now. He likes to sleep late in the morning."

"Have you told him yet?" Ricardo asked.

"That I'm leaving? No, I haven't. *I do* need to do that." Gregg frowned.

"Will he go back to couch surfing in La Chorrera?"

"I guess. I don't know. I need to talk with him. I asked Ted whether he could just stay here while I was gone if I paid the rent, but Ted said no."

Although Ricardo was glad about that, he only said, "Really?"

"Yeah, Ted's a racist, you know. He won't rent to any of the locals. He only rents to gringos. He flat came out and told me that," Gregg said.

"Really? What did he say about Luciano staying here this past month?" Ricardo asked.

"He didn't say anything, but I didn't ask. I didn't think it was any of his business."

"Well, the lease does say 'no extended visitor stays,'" said Ricardo.

"But it doesn't define it, so I didn't ask. Live and let live, that's my motto. But I think when I come back, I'll find a different place to live. This place isn't that friendly."

"Yeah..." Ricardo said, "but I like it because it's safe. I mean, I was all against gated communities when I first came to Panama years ago, but I don't even notice the fence and the barbed wire now. I've gotten used to the gate, and used to feeling secure here. Ted says no one's ever been robbed here."

"Yeah, that's true," Gregg said.

"Are you going to keep in touch with Luciano while you're gone?" Ricardo asked.

"Oh yes," Gregg said. "We're already Facebook friends."

Ricardo laughed. "He's on Facebook? That's funny."

"Why? It's free," Gregg said.

"True... I guess I'm just not up on technology," Ricardo said.

"Aren't you on Facebook?" Gregg asked.

"No, I'm not," Ricardo lied. In fact, Ricardo was on Facebook, and had been on it for almost eight years, but not under his real name. He had opened a Facebook account under his pen name when he first started writing and publishing his books. At that time, he was working as a lawyer for a small law firm in Hamburg, New York, doing probate cases, and he felt that he couldn't jeopardize his career with the fact that he was writing adult books and short stories that contained a lot of sex, bondage, and dark themes. Eight years ago, he had no idea that his books would sell. Once they did, he had no reason to change his pen name or his Facebook page. In fact, his publisher helped him design a website under his pseudonym that linked to his Facebook page and to the publisher's website to help promote his books. Ricardo liked keeping his personal life separate from his author life. It didn't make any difference anymore after he retired and moved to Panama, of course. He did book tours, interviews, and readings back in the States. It was part of his publishing contract. But he still liked the day-to-day anonymity of using his real name for things like traveling, or renting apartments. He would only share himself as a writer to close friends, and aside from Alison and a few others in the States, he had no close friends. When he first rented the apartment in Villa Rosario, he had told Ted that he did some freelance writing, but left it at that, and Ted didn't inquire further. No one at the Island knew his pseudonym or the types of books that he wrote. In fact, no one in Panama knew. He liked it that way, and certainly wasn't going to reveal any of that to Gregg.

"I guess I'm behind the times, Gregg. I don't do Facebook, Twitter, or any of that other shit," Ricardo said.

"Oh, you should. I have about five hundred friends on Facebook," Gregg said.

Ricardo believed that was probably true, but changed the subject.

"Are you going to come back to Panama?"

"I think so. I'm not sure," Gregg said. "I have a friend in Barcelona who wants me to come and visit next month, but I just don't know. I've had such a good time down here, and it's easy to get back to the States from here."

"And what about Luciano? Will you take him back under your wing when you come back?"

"Yeah, no, I don't think so. I mean, he's a beautiful boy, but I think it's time for him to move on. I've really done enough for him," Gregg said.

Ricardo thought to himself that what Gregg really meant was that he was growing tired of Luciano.

Gregg continued, "Luckily, I booked this flight back to the States months ago, so I have the perfect excuse. The other day, I suggested to Luciano that he should go back to La Chorrera, but he didn't want to, and he talked me into letting him stay."

"Well, no shit," Ricardo said. "It's pleasant here. You're good company, and he's probably eating better than he ever has in his life."

"Yeah, well..." Gregg said, "all good things have to come to an end."

# Chapter 15: Darren

When Jonathan was off to Sosua on his "fishing expeditions" (as he liked to call them), Carl was left at the Island to fend for himself, which is when Carl would seek out Darren. Darren wasn't around much during the day. He was one of the few expats who actually did something for the community of Villa Rosario, volunteering at the local community center near the park teaching art classes. Ricardo admired him for that, although he recognized that for Darren it was just a continuation of the job he had retired from. Darren had been an art teacher in various high schools in Phoenix for his whole career, but then he got hit with a triple-whammy of a bitter divorce, bankruptcy, and budget cuts in the school district that doomed his job. So he decided it was time to retire (or, to be more accurate, it was decided for him). But Darren explained one time to Ricardo that he simply couldn't give up teaching art.

"I thought I was sick of it. But after I retired, I realized that I missed it," Darren explained to Ricardo one evening over a beer down at the table on the patio. "I realized it wasn't the teaching I was sick of. It was all the bureaucracy that was being foisted on us. When that 'no child left behind' crap started, we all had to start doing performance reviews, daily student evaluations, and lesson plans. Jesus fucking Christ, what a load of crap! I'm an art teacher, but I was spending more time filling out paperwork—describing *what* I was going to teach, *how* I was going to teach it, *what* each student was going to learn, *how* that learning unit was going to fit into each student's learning plan, *how* I was going to evaluate the learning—than I actually spent *teaching art*.

Jesus fucking Christ! We're talking art here! That's the whole point about art—you don't evaluate it, you just do it. But down here, it's different; I can just go into the community center and teach. I never have to fill out any paperwork. The kids love it; I love it. I wished I had moved here years ago. I guess that's the one thing I can thank *her* for—forcing me to move here."

The 'her' that Darren was referring to; the woman he always referred to; the one he could never stop talking about; as Ricardo very quickly discovered, was his ex-wife Christy. He had nothing good to say about her, and he said it often. He'd come downstairs to the patio table every night about six, with a six-pack of beer, which he'd share with any listener at the table, and after a new minutes of small talk, he would find a way to launch into a story of how Christy had ruined his life, leaving him financially and emotionally bankrupt. The beers would guarantee a nightly audience, and Darren had a never-ending supply of stories.

Ricardo did notice that on those infrequent times that Jonathan was in town and at the table, Darren wouldn't come out from his apartment to join the group. Ricardo guessed that Darren didn't like Jonathan because they were both competing for the same audience. And although Jonathan's stories always included graphic recounting of various sexual encounters, the crowd at the table was bigger when Darren was there, because Darren always brought beer (which Jonathan never did). But the schedule of nightly performances pleased Carl, because it meant that he always had someone to sit next to, and listen to, and ask questions of. The first time that Ricardo witnessed Carl's questions, he almost had the impression that Carl was interviewing Darren.

"So, did she get the condo, then?" Carl asked.

"Fuck, no!" Darren said. "We were so upside down in that dump. No, she was no dummy. She tried to get the judge to give it to me, but the judge saw through that. The place was only worth maybe eighty thousand, and we owed almost a hundred-fifty on it."

"Wow," Carl said. "Was that because of the real estate crash?"

"Fuck no... well, in part, yes. But really, it was because she kept making me refinance it over and over, so she could have money for clothes and vacations and her various projects. Hell, we must have refinanced it five times in the three years we owned it. The real estate bubble was part of it because the mortgage company kept re-appraising it for more and more money. Phoenix real estate was hot back then. But it was her fucking projects—did I tell you about the time that she got on a vitamin and supplement kick, and wanted to open up some kind of herbal franchise? Herb Life or Herb Light... fuck, I can't remember the name, but she plowed ten grand into buying supplies. It was some kind of Tupperware business model—she was going to sell vitamins and supplements out of our condo. Vitamin parties she called them. Fuck."

"What happened with that?" Carl asked.

"She fucking lost interest, that's what the fuck happened! She tried one or two parties and realized it was a lot of work, and that fucking Christy, work was for other people... so we were stuck with boxes and boxes of vitamins. Ten grand, down the fucking drain."

"So what happened with the condo?" Carl asked.

"Well, we both moved out, and just stopped making payments. I ended up filing for bankruptcy. I know she filed her paperwork, but my attorney told me he had heard she never completed it, so I don't know what happened to her debt, and I really don't care. As soon as I got my discharge papers all approved, I took my pension and moved down here. Best move I ever made," Darren said, "Want another beer, Carl?"

"Yeah, sure, thanks," Carl said.

Ricardo was listening to all this and thought it might be nice to hear about a different subject, so he asked, "How are the art classes going downtown, Darren?"

"Oh... fine... they're fine... they're good... and another thing Carl, remember I told you how she made such a big deal at the divorce hearing about getting our dog, how it meant everything to her, that she needed it to cope emotionally with the divorce?"

"Yeah?" Carl said.

"Well, I found out later that about a week after the divorce, she took that dog down to the pound. To the pound! She just did it so I couldn't have him, 'cause she knew I loved that dog. As soon as I found out, I ran down to the pound, but by that time, he had already been adopted out. Can you imagine? How could someone do that?"

"Yeah," said Carl. "What a bitch!"

Ricardo thought to himself, *Well, you married her, Darren.* But he kept that thought to himself, and instead said, "Well, gentlemen, it's time for me to turn in. Thank you for the beer, Darren. See you all later." As he walked back to his apartment, he made a mental note not to hang around the patio table too often. It was a shame, he thought, what bitterness does to a man. He had seen some of Darren's paintings. The guy was a good painter, probably a good teacher, but view of life was just bitter.

# Chapter 16: Albert and Louis

Albert and Louis made up the last two residents of the Island, and Ricardo knew the least about them. In fact, he had never met Louis. According to Ted, Louis kept his apartment year-round, but lived most of the time in the States. Ricardo thought this was a good deal for Ted: full rent with no upkeep. Evidently, Louis had money, because he would come to Panama three or four times a year, stay in the apartment for a week or two, and then leave. According to Dan, Louis just liked leaving all his clothes there so he could travel light. Dan also said that Louis also kept a timeshare in Hawaii and Colorado, and had some place in Spain. That was all Ricardo knew about Louis.

On the other hand, he had seen Albert a few times, and had even said hello, but only knew a little more about him than he knew about Louis. Albert was the oldest resident at the Island. Dan said Albert was about eighty-two, and that he had lived at the apartment building for almost ten years. Albert lived upstairs, at the opposite corner from Ted. Louis' apartment was next to Albert's. Then came Jonathan's apartment, then Dan's, and finally Ted's corner apartment.

Dan claimed that Albert used to be quite active once, but now his health wasn't so good. On rare occasions, Ricardo would see Albert walking around the garden. He looked frail.

"He stays inside his apartment most of the day," Dan had explained to Ricardo once. "I rarely see him. Ted checks up on him each day, I guess to see if he's still alive. I know he has his groceries delivered. Ted told me that some doctor came out once and also checked on him. I know he takes a lot of meds, but I don't know what for. I suppose he's just waiting to die."

"That's sad," Ricardo said. "I wouldn't want to end up like that."

"Shit, dude," Dan said. "*We all* end up like that. I mean, I'd rather spend my last days in an apartment in Panama than stuck inside some nursing home back in the States. The smell of those places is enough to kill you."

"No. I meant being alone. He never has any visitors," Ricardo said.

"Well, like I said, we all end up like that. Shit, if any of us had had real friends back in the States, we would never have become expats down here."

Ricardo didn't think of himself or any of the Island's residents as true expats, but he did agree with Dan's assessment that everyone at the Island was, in some way, an outsider, cut off from the usual community of friends. Even Jonathan and Gregg, the two most gregarious residents, despite all their chatty ways, and claims of many friends, seemed to Ricardo to be desperately lonely men, simply moving from conquest to conquest. Of course, Ricardo worried he had the same tendencies, but at least he felt like he had a few real friends in Alison, Miguel, and Alejandro. But of all the residents, Ricardo thought that only Darren had potential to establish roots here, to find a community. If Darren could just find a local Panamanian woman to love, someone to help him get over Christy, Ricardo thought... but then of course, he had to smile to himself. That was the same thing that everyone thinks about lonely men: If they could just find a nice girl to settle down with, they would be happy. Ricardo knew that just wasn't true.

# Chapter 17: Eve

"Tell me about Eve," Alison said, out of the blue. It was late in the evening, about eight days into her visit at the Island. She and Ricardo were lying naked in bed, the thin top blanket and sheet crumpled to the side of the bed, the ceiling fan on high, cooling them down from making love, and they were just cuddling and talking. Alison had gotten up to dig through her purse to get her vaporizer, and had returned to the bed to smoke. Ricardo didn't like that she smoked e-cigarettes, but he couldn't complain about the smell or any taste on her breath, like he could back when she smoked regular cigarettes. She had almost quit cigarettes completely when e-cigarettes came along. She was just going to use them to help her quit, she said at the time. That was several years ago.

They had been talking about old relationships, and people they had known, when Alison suddenly brought up Eve.

"Why?" Ricardo said quickly.

"Because I want to know," Alison said. "You were in love with her, weren't you?"

"I don't remember," Ricardo said.

"Oh, come on! It's been over for years. Don't be such a pussy. Tell me."

"God, you can be demanding," Ricardo said, and kissed her on the cheek. "Yeah, I think I did love her. It was just one of those fucked-up deals. I really thought she was going to divorce her husband—they had been separated for two years, living apart. But, I guess marriage is a funny

81

thing. It just pulls you back in. They had been married, fuck, I don't know, eighteen or twenty years, you know, and had kids together. Even after two years apart, she took him back. Last time I heard, they were still together."

"How much did you love her?"

Ricardo hesitated a minute and then said, "A lot."

"Enough to marry her?" Alison asked.

"Jesus! You should have been a lawyer... I don't know... maybe, but I was already planning on moving here when she and I met, so I don't know how that would have played out... Why all the questions?"

"Oh, no reason," Alison shrugged and put her vaporizer on the nightstand.

"Bullshit, Alison. Why all the questions?"

"I was wondering if you'd ever marry again," she said.

"Oh, *that*... I don't know. You know me, I'm not exactly faithful."

"No," she said, "actually I don't know. I've read your books, but I know you bullshit a lot."

"You know I was divorced twice," he said.

"I know. Anyway, tell me about Eve. Were you faithful to her?"

"What? For the six to eight months we were together? Yeah, I guess, at least there were no other women."

"Any other men?" she asked.

"Well, no other relationships... casual sex with men is different. It's... well, if I said I don't remember sex with any other men, I would be telling the truth... that I don't *remember* it, because casual sex with men is not meant to be remembered. That's why it so often happens in the closet, so everyone can forget it and pretend it never happened. I'm not saying I didn't go to the bathhouses while she and I dated. I can't say that. But, if your question is, do I remember cheating on her, my answer is no, I do not remember ever cheating on her or wanting to cheat on her. She kept me pretty occupied."

"Was she a better lover than me?" Alison asked.

"Stop it!" Ricardo exclaimed. He sat up in bed. "How old are you? Don't you know never to ask that question? It's an impossible question... But... there is always only one answer.... and that is..." he paused and smiled, "no one's better than you, my love."

"Ha," Alison snorted. "Do you want to hear about my lovers?"

"Fuck no! Jesus fucking Christ, Alison. That's a worse sin than asking a man who's better... is talking about *your* former lovers."

"Well, I know all about yours, plus all the whores," she said.

"That's only because I write about them, Alison. I don't talk about them."

"Well, I read what you write, so I know about you."

"Hmmmph," grunted Ricardo.

"Just like you look at my paintings," she said.

"I don't get the comparison," he said. "I see beautiful paintings, I mean, I know you created them, and I'm proud of you, and I think you're talented, but the paintings stand on their own. A person doesn't need to know you to appreciate them," Ricardo said.

"But you know me, and you know me and my history through my paintings," she said.

"I'm not sure I follow," he said.

"Well, remember those nude paintings I did before the elephant series?" she asked.

"Yeah."

"Well, remember I was dating that guy David?"

Ricardo covered his ears and starting chanting, "Ya ya ya ya ya ya I don't want to know!"

Alison laughed and pushed a pillow over his head.

"You're so silly," she said. "You want to sound all grown up, but you're just a kid."

"All men are children," Ricardo said. "*Puer aeternus*, the ancient Romans called it—eternal youth. We're all just little Peter Pans."

"Yeah you are. You, with your lost boys," she laughed.

"Well, I prefer to think of myself as Phallus in Wonderland, baby," he said, slipping his hand between her legs. "Can I fall down your rabbit hole one more time tonight, baby?"

# Chapter 18:   Confrontations

It was a couple of days after deciding not to go to Jenny's that Ricardo overheard the confrontation between Paul, Ted, and Dan. It was late morning, and Ricardo was sitting inside his apartment typing away on his computer at his little desk. The sun had reached that certain point in the sky where it was higher than the bamboo-covered concrete wall that surrounded the Island, but lower than the shade that the patio eaves provided. At this point every day, the sun beamed directly into Ricardo's window. In another hour, it would be blocked by the patio eaves. But for that hour every day, Ricardo had to draw the blinds to block the sun while he wrote. His door was open, of course, for the breeze. He had just closed the blinds when he heard Ted come down to visit Paul. Ricardo didn't think anything of it and continued typing. But after about ten minutes, he could hear raised voices.

"I don't care, Ted, I just want those fags outta here!" Paul was saying.

Ricardo stopped typing and started listening. Paul's voice was getting louder.

"I have to walk by his apartment to go anywhere, and every time I do, he and that kid are stretched out on the bed together."

Ricardo knew what Paul was talking about, but also knew that Paul was exaggerating. The Island studio apartments were small. There really wasn't much room for a guest and a resident to sit and talk. And yes, Luciano usually was usually stretched out on Gregg's bed, checking his cell phone or playing video games on Gregg's iPad while Gregg was talking to him. And yes, Gregg's door was usually open, as were his blinds, so it was possible for anyone who walked by to see in. But Gregg usually sat in a chair, or stood and cooked, or maybe sat on the edge of the bed while he talked to Luciano. Ricardo had never seen Gregg lying down on the bed next to Luciano. He knew that Gregg was too smart for that; he would have closed the door and the window blinds. But it was clear that the appearance of a gay relationship between the older Gregg and the younger Luciano was very upsetting to Paul.

"Look, Paul. There's nothing I can do about it," Ted was saying. "He pays his rent just like you do, and he's allowed to have guests, just like you are."

"The difference is, I close my door!" Paul shouted. "You can make him close his door!"

Now Ricardo could hear Ted raising his voice in frustration. "For what, Paul? Every time he has someone over? I can't do that. As long as nobody's naked and everyone's of a legal age, there's nothing I can do."

"Goddamn it, Ted! You're the owner. Of course you can do something about it! He's on a month-to-month lease. Just tell him to take his faggy friend and get the fuck out!"

"I'm done with this discussion, Paul," and Ted stormed out of Paul's apartment. But Paul followed him, still trying to argue.

"Look, Ted. I've been here for seven years. I'm a long-term resident. He's only been here a few months. I have certain rights!" Paul was saying.

It sounded like Paul was following Ted upstairs to Ted's apartment. Ricardo hoped that Gregg and Luciano weren't home to hear this. He had heard them go out a few hours ago, and hoped they hadn't returned. Ricardo stood up, went over to his screen door and listened. He could hear Ted and Paul upstairs, arguing up on Ted's patio. Ricardo stepped outside, being careful not to let the screen door slam. He stood there on his patio, under the eaves, listening to the argument continue upstairs.

"Look, Paul," Ted was saying, "I treat everyone the same. As long as people keep their business quiet inside their apartment, I don't interfere."

"But I *can see* them!"

"Paul, remember that guy who lived next to you, where Ricardo lives now? Remember he complained about smelling your dope? Remember? He said he had smoke allergies and wanted me to make you stop, remember? And I told him if he didn't like it, he could move. So he moved. And I'm telling *you* the same thing—if you don't like it, you can move. It's none of my business what two people do inside their apartment."

Just then Ricardo heard Dan come out of his apartment and asked what was going on.

"You boys having a lovers' quarrel?" Dan asked. Ricardo almost smiled. Dan sounded just like a cop trying to diffuse a domestic quarrel.

"You stay out of this," Paul said. "This is between Ted and me"

"Not when it's this loud and in front of my door, Paul." Dan said. "Now what's going on?"

"Paul is upset that Gregg has that boy here," Ted said.

"Oh? Why is that, Paul? You have something against queerboys?" Dan asked. Dan's tone was slightly mocking, cajoling.

"Well... well... yeah!" Paul sputtered. "Yeah, I *do!* I don't want them shoving it in my face. Every time I walk by that apartment, that boy is lying on his bed."

"If that's true, so what?" asked Dan.

"And that fag is lying down with him."

"And if that's true, so what?" Dan reiterated.

"Well, they look like they're going to start fucking or something."

"And if that's true, so what?"

"Well, that's disgusting!"

But now Dan's tone turned serious and direct. "So, it's disgusting. Don't watch! Get over it, Paul. Life is too short. None of us moved down here to be upset. Gregg's not a long-

87

term tenant. He's going back to the States soon. Everyone knows that. He'll be gone soon. Let it go. It's not worth it."

Ricardo tried to hear more, but the voices were calming down, and he couldn't make out all the words. He figured that the discussion was about over, so he stepped back into his apartment. He sat down at his desk and thought about this weird outburst from Paul. Just then he heard Paul walking by. Apparently, Paul was still unaware that Ricardo was there. Either that or he didn't care, because as he walked by, Ricardo heard him swearing under his breath "Fucking liberal assholes!" before disappearing into his apartment and slamming the door.

# Chapter 19:   Pesto

A few nights later, Ricardo invited Alejandro over for dinner. He was telling him about the confrontation he had witnessed. Because it was the weekend, and Paul had gone to Panama City (as was his normal custom) and Gregg had taken Luciano to La Chorrera to have dinner and see a movie, Ricardo felt safe inviting Alejandro over. Ricardo was not worried about offending Paul, but he knew that if Gregg had seen Alejandro at Ricardo's apartment, Gregg would have invited himself and Luciano over to join them, and Ricardo didn't want that.

"I know that Paul," Alejandro was saying. "I know everybody. He comes into the store and never says hello to anyone. None of the cashiers like him. He is never friendly. I'm not surprised he is a hater. He is a very unhappy man."

"Well, I'm always amazed at homophobia," Ricardo said.

"It's common. Many gays have it too." Alejandro said. "What are you making? It smells good."

"It's a salmon pesto pasta. I found a jar of pesto in the gringo section of your store today. Never seen it available here before, so I bought it so I could make this."

Alejandro laughed. "Jes, we stock that shelf with things only gringos would buy. It was expensive, no?"

"Yes, it was."

Alejandro laughed again. "We charge extra for stuff on that shelf. What else are you putting in it?"

"Well, there's the salmon, and garlic, of course. And lots of red peppers. And I mix in tiny pieces of broccoli. That's what gives it a good flavor. Then I'll add the pasta when it's done, with some butter, and the pesto."

"You are a good cook, señor." Alejandro said, smiling.

"Thank you, señor," Ricardo said. "I like to cook."

"Is there much garlic in the food?" asked Alejandro.

"Yes, there is. I like garlic."

"Well, then I should kiss you before we eat," said Alejandro, and he walked over to where Ricardo was standing stirring the pasta, and kissed him on the lips. It was a good kiss, and Ricardo liked it.

"Well," said Ricardo, "we'll both be eating garlic, so we can probably kiss after dinner too."

"Okay," said Alejandro with a smile, and rubbed Ricardo's back. "We will do that then."

# Chapter 20:   Jenny

A few nights later, as Ricardo approached the door to Jenny's brothel, he thought about what Miguel had recommended the previous week: that he should go to Jenny's and then go to the bathhouse and then see if he still missed Alison. He hadn't made it to the bathhouse this week, but he did have sex with Alejandro, so he figured that counted even better than the bathhouse.

Jenny greeted him as he stepped inside. As usual, she was nicely dressed. They sat and chatted awhile. Ricardo had a new respect for her because of what Miguel had told him. She offered him coffee or tea, and he accepted a cup of tea.

They talked about La Chorrera and how it seemed to be changing. Ricardo mentioned he had seen a few graffiti tags on some walls on the edge of town. Jenny said she had seen it too, and did not like what it represented. Juvenile crime had always been a problem in Panama. But over the past thirty years, as the drug trafficking increased, gangs had taken hold. It used to be that the Colombians and other drug traffickers would simply fly their product into Mexico and then ship it overland into the U.S., but joint police operations between the DEA and the Mexican government had all but shut down illicit drug flights into Mexico. U.S. spy planes monitored the skies high above Mexico, and any small plane coming from South America was tracked. As soon as it landed in Mexico, the Mexican police were there to search it. It was a very effective program, but only effective in shutting down air flights as a method of transportation.

The cartels simply reverted to using boats or shipping drugs overland. And when the drugs moved through Panama, the cartels needed local help in warehousing and moving the drugs. So they turned to the gangs, and they paid them in drugs, which the gangs would then sell to turn into cash. That caused the gangs to expand their territories, looking for new clients to sell drugs to. La Chorrera had historically been too far from Panama City to be affected by gangs, but the new graffiti indicated that this might be changing.

"I don't like it, don Ricardo," Jenny was saying. "I saw how this same thing destroyed neighborhoods in Panama City. When the young men get into gangs, they never leave, except to go to jail, or in a coffin. My girls, they tell me how they are approached by teenagers who try to sell them drugs. It's a bad thing. If I find out one of my girls is using, I fire her on the spot. But my girls are good; they tell me everything."

"I've always liked it here, Jenny. You run a clean house."

"Only the best. I am always here. If some man comes to the door, and he is drunk, I do not let him in. I say 'come back when you are sober'. I do not like drunk clients or rude clients. We are here for love, not for just sex."

Ricardo smiled. He liked the impossible thought that a brothel existed for love and not for just sex.

"By the way, don Ricardo, I have a very nice new girl here now. I think you would like her. She is local but tall and thin. You know, the local men, they like the girls short and plump, but I know you. You like them thin, like boys."

Ricardo laughed out loud. "Ah Jenny, you devil you! You do know me. What's her name?"

"Magali. I think in English it means pearl, but she is a dark pearl. She is very nice. Do you want to meet her?"

"Yes, of course."

Jenny's place operated different than most brothels. In every other brothel that Ricardo had ever been to, the girls lined up and the customer picked the one he wanted. Ricardo supposed that such a system forced the girls to pretty themselves up as much as possible, to compete with the other girls, because the prettiest ones, or the ones who acted the sexiest when the man was choosing, made the most money. But at Jenny's it was different. Jenny never let the girls line up. Jenny would chat with a customer, then Jenny would make a selection and have that one girl come out. If the customer didn't like that particular girl, Jenny would not offer a second choice, but tell him to come back another time. Ricardo had asked her about her method once, and she had explained to him that it spread the money evenly, eliminated any fighting between the girls, and that most customers went with the girl that Jenny picked. Ricardo certainly had always been happy with Jenny's selections.

Ricardo was also very secure with Jenny's health standards. She had a nurse physically inspect the girls once a week and administer throat and vaginal swabs to check for syphilis and gonorrhea. And Jenny was hyper-vigilant about HIV. She required every girl to use condoms for every sex act, every time. She once showed Ricardo her stockpile of rapid-test HIV throat swab kits. Each girl had to take that test each week as well. Once a month the visiting nurse took blood samples for a complete STD screen. Jenny's had a reputation, even as far away as Panama City, as the cleanest, safest brothel in Panama, and she had a loyal following of regulars. Some of the local men said they didn't like Jenny's because the prices were high. But Ricardo was always willing to pay for the extra security.

Jenny picked up the phone, dialed a number, and asked Magali to come downstairs. A few minutes later, Magali appeared. She was, as Jenny had described, tall and thin, with small breasts, very boyish looking. Her dark hair was cut short and straight, and fell just below her jaw line. She was dark but with a very clear complexion, and her eyes fit Jenny's metaphor of dark pearl. Ricardo liked her immediately.

After introductions and some small chit-chat, Jenny looked at Ricardo, nodded towards Magali, and raised her eyebrows to ask if he approved. "Yes, Jenny," Ricardo said. "Thank you. She is very beautiful."

Magali smiled and lowered her head. Jenny gave another gesture, and Magali took Ricardo's hand and led him upstairs.

The rooms at Jenny's brothel were small but elegant. Whereas the rooms in most brothels just had a bed, the rooms at Jenny's had a bed, plus two comfortable chairs for sitting, a coat rack with hangers for clothes, and a shower stall with glass doors built right into the room, complete with fresh towels.

Ricardo and Magali sat down in the chairs to settle on terms. Ricardo knew the basic menu: $200 for an hour, and $500 for all night. Jenny's place was not cheap, but Ricardo appreciated why.

He looked at Magali while they were talking. He liked her high cheekbones, her dark eyes, and her smile. It was not just that she was pretty, but she had a delicate, non-hurried, almost shy way about her. He felt tender about her the moment he met her. Usually, he would have only purchased an hour of time, but somehow tonight, he felt like sleeping beside her and waking up with her. This was something he would never consider doing at any other brothel. In fact, he had never done it at any brothel in Panama, but somehow, tonight it felt right. He knew Jenny's was safe. So he told Magali that he would like to stay the night. She smiled. Ricardo hoped that somehow his request did actually please her. He paid her and said he was going to take a shower while she took the money downstairs.

He was just drying off when Magali came back in, wearing a white bathrobe. She smiled shyly, slipped out of the robe and stepped into the shower. Ricardo watched her shower. Long legs, dark coffee skin, tight butt, small breasts, dark nipples. "Absolutely beautiful," he thought to himself, and finished drying himself.

She stepped out of the shower, and he handed her a clean towel. She gave him a little kiss on the lips. He pulled the sheets back as she dried herself off, and then they both lay down together. She slipped into his arms easily, like a lover, and they began to kiss.

It wasn't until many weeks later, after the tumultuous events that followed the day after that night, that Ricardo had time to reflect on his night with Magali. And there was much to reflect on, because he had made love with Alejandro just a few nights before, and Alejandro was just as handsome as Magali was beautiful. And somehow, making love to two very similar, but genetically different, creatures highlighted the duality of Ricardo's nature.

When it came to a gender preference for sex or for making love (the two often being different), Ricardo considered himself "eclectic". He hated the term "bisexual". It was as useless a term as "stereo" was in describing music. But he always found that sex was completely different depending on the gender. The activities might be similar, but the feeling was different. With Alejandro, there was a lot of teasing, role-playing, heated touching, but always stopping before either one came. The joy in the sex came from the stimulation. Both he and Alejandro wore cock rings, to keep themselves hard, and both he and Alejandro enjoyed sucking and being sucked, so they would naturally alternate, raising the other's passion up, licking the head of each other's cock then taking it deep in their mouth and throat. When one needed to cool down, he would suck the other one's cock. Occasionally there was some domination role-playing, where one would hold the other down by the wrists sitting on his chest, forcing his cock into the other's mouth, fucking his mouth. This type of playful male lovemaking went on for almost two hours, until in some type of mutually understood moment, they both masturbated each other and came at the same time, shooting out long strings of white cum.

But with women, lovemaking was simply different. Depending on the woman, it might be rough or gentle; it might involve role-playing; there certainly was the same controlled building of tension; but in some way that Ricardo could never describe, the sexuality, the carnality, the bestiality of the act was simply different. With Magali, there was more face-to-face kissing, and Ricardo enjoyed the simple act of running his hands down the small of her back, grasping each of her butt cheeks in each hand and pulling her close to him. The act of full body contact, limbs intertwined, with a woman, had its own eroticism, as if the electrical current was being dispelled across the entire body. With men, the eroticism of full body contact was the thrill of feeling cock touching cock, as if the electrical energy was gushing in just that area. Ricardo never could understand it. But with men, sex was intense because he knew it was going to end, but with women, sex was intense because he didn't want it to ever end.

Because he knew he had all night, Ricardo enjoyed his time with Magali slowly. They kissed. He nibbled on her ear. He cupped each breast in his hands and rolled over on top of her. He eased his way down her body and stopped to lick, kiss, suckle, and gently bite at each of her long dark nipples. He ran his hand up between her legs, holding his two fingers apart and traced each of her two pussy lips, squeezing the lips together and then apart. He gently massaged her clit. He reached back to grab her ass, pressing the heel of his palm against her clit. He eased his way down her body, reaching that sweet pussy and nibbled away while reaching up and playing with her breasts. She in turn played with his balls, gently rasping her fingernails over them, running her fingers up and down his cock while lying on top of him, then rolling off in such a way that her breasts ended up at his mouth level. Finally, she took a condom from a drawer in the night stand, rolled it over his cock and sucked him while twisting his balls. Then she crawled over him, on top of him, and slid his cock up into her pussy and gently rocked to and fro. When it got too intense, Ricardo pulled out, and rolled so his back was facing her. She laughed and wrapped her arms around him. He could feel her wet pussy against his ass.

Finally, after about an hour of playing and teasing, he couldn't stand it anymore. He climbed on top her, entered her, raising each of her legs to his shoulders, grasping each buttock in his hands lifting her ass up and her pelvis into him, and fucked her hard. He came, cried out, gave a couple more thrusts, and then toppled over on his side. She tightened her legs and arms around him and pulled him close.

After a few minutes, he reached down, wrapped his thumb and first finger around the base of his cock to hold the condom in place, and eased out of her. She reached over to the nightstand and grabbed two small towels. One she wrapped over his cock with the condom still on it, and one she placed between her legs. Then she wrapped her legs and arms around him once more, and they both just lay there quietly.

Just before he fell asleep, she reached down and grabbed the towel that was around his cock, and pulled it off in such a way that it carried the condom with it. She got up, placed the towel in a bin, turned off the light, came back to bed, and pulled the sheet over both of them.

Ricardo woke up several times that night. He could hear her gently breathing. He could smell the scent of sex. He leaned over to her shoulder and smelled her. She smelled good. He fell back to sleep, hoping he wouldn't snore.

When he woke up the next morning, he was lying on his back, and Magali was by his side. He looked over at her. Her eyes were open. She smiled. She nodded her head down. He looked down and saw that he had a morning erection. It wasn't a sexual erection, but he could make it one. He nodded. She grabbed another condom from the nightstand and rolled it on his cock. He took her from behind this time, not so much for the variety but out of courtesy because he hadn't brushed his teeth. It was a morning quickie, purely for his pleasure, but it was good.

Later, after his shower, he tipped her a hundred dollars and thanked her honestly for a wonderful night and told her he would ask for her the next time he came back.

On the bus ride back to Villa Rosario that morning, Ricardo was still floating in some type of post-coital bliss.

That was a beautiful time, an incredible time, he thought. But then he began to think of Alison. He knew better than to compare lovers, but he also knew that, as tender and grateful as he felt to Magali, he was also missing Alison. Her style and carnality were different from Magali's, but he had a history with her. She was a friend as well as a lover. He knew Alison. They could talk about things. Maybe with time, he might get to know Magali, but right now he knew nothing about her other than her lovemaking. He thought about Alejandro. He had a history with Alejandro, though nowhere like the years he had with Alison. He tried to put all these crazy-making comparisons out of his mind, but he did miss Alison. Damn that Miguel, he thought.

# Chapter 21: According to Ted

The bus that Ricardo caught in front of Jenny's in La Chorrera dropped him off in Villa Rosario about four blocks from the Island. Ricardo saw the police cars and flashing blue lights as he was walking up the hill from the bus stop. "Uh oh," he thought. "I bet Albert died." But as he got closer, and realized how many police cars were there, he wondered what was going on.

According to Ted, it was Carl who first saw the bloody footprints. As Ted told it, Carl came knocking on his door early that morning, saying there were bare footprints all in red like blood, leaving Gregg's apartment. Carl thought Gregg had cut his foot bad, so he knocked on Gregg's door but there was no answer. That's when Carl went upstairs to Ted's apartment and woke him up. Ted came to the door in his underwear.

"God damn it, Carl, what time is it?" Ted barked, but when Carl told him what he had seen, Ted snapped awake, grabbed a bathrobe and his ring of master keys and followed Ted downstairs. At first he was pissed off—he thought it would be hard to get dried blood off the concrete walkway outside of the apartments. He looked at the footprints and cursed out loud. But after knocking on Gregg's door and also getting no answer, it began to dawn on him that he might have a bigger problem. He opened the lock with his key, pushed the door open while calling Gregg's name, and then he looked inside. He gasped, and took a step back. It seemed to take all his air to say to Carl, "Call the police." Carl just stood there, dumbfounded. Then Ted yelled at him, "Call the fucking police!" and Carl scurried off to his apartment to get his cell phone. Ted started to step inside to see if Gregg was still alive, but one look at the number of knife wounds in Gregg's back, and the amount of blood on the bed and floor, told him that even if Gregg were alive, there would be nothing that Ted could do for him. Better to wait for the police.

When Ricardo arrived, the police were in full swarm. There was a crowd standing around the gate to the apartment building. Ricardo saw one of the neighbors that he knew standing on the side and asked him, "Qué pasó?" The neighbor shook his head and shrugged his shoulders and said that he had only heard someone was dead. Ricardo then squeezed his way to the front of the crowd and tried to talk to the police there. At first they told him to stay away, but when they realized he lived there, they pulled him inside the gates. Two policemen grilled him about where he had been since yesterday evening. Ricardo later learned that yesterday evening around nine was the last time anyone had seen Gregg alive. They didn't tell him that Gregg had been murdered, but given the number of police and the intensity of their questions, Ricardo knew that something bad had happened. But he also knew that, luckily, he could account for his time. He then told them he had been at Jenny's for the entire night. He didn't know Jenny's phone number but one of the cops obviously did. They made him sit in one of the patrol cars for about thirty minutes while they called Jenny. Evidently Jenny vouched for him, because one of the officers came over to the car and told him he was free to go.

Ricardo walked up the steps towards the front of the apartment building, where he saw Carl, Ted, Paul, and Darren standing together talking on the grassy area near the patio. The front of the building and the sidewalk was blocked off with yellow police tape. Over near Gregg's door, Ricardo saw Dan talking to a group of police officers.

Ricardo walked up to the group and asked Ted, "What happened?"

But it was Paul who answered. "That little faggot killed your friend, that's what happened! Look at his footprints!"

Ricardo looked down at the sidewalk where Paul was pointing. The sight of the bloody footprints made him feel queasy. Ricardo looked at Paul, said nothing, then looked at Ted.

"Well, we don't know anything for sure," Ted said. "But that's what it looks like. Gregg's door was locked, the police can't find the key, and there was no sign of a break-in. It looks like his roommate stabbed him to death."

"Shit," Ricardo said.

Ted then filled Ricardo in on how he and Carl had discovered Gregg's body. Ted described how Gregg was lying naked on the bed with one leg dangling off the edge, and both arms up by his face. His back was facing the apartment door so that what Ted saw was about ten to fifteen stab wounds in Gregg's back and buttocks. Ted seemed truly shaken.

"It was ungodly horrible, Ricardo. There was blood everywhere," Ted said.

"And the footprints?" Ricardo asked, "did they come from inside the apartment?"

"Yeah," said Ted, "there was a big pool of blood and they seem to start from there."

Just then Dan walked up to the group.

"Ricardo," Dan said, "can I talk to you for a minute?"

"Sure," Ricardo said, and he and Dan walked away from the group.

"Listen, Ricardo," Dan said, "I don't know if Gregg was a close friend of yours or not. If he was, I'm sorry."

"We were just neighbors," Ricardo said. "But still, he didn't deserve this."

"I know. Look, this is kind of a big deal here, because this kind of thing doesn't happen in Villa Rosario, especially not to gringos. The cops want to solve this thing fast. I'm kinda friends with José Fernando, who's like the police chief here. He doesn't speak English, so I offered to help. Between you and me, they're in over their heads, walking all over the crime scene and everything. But let me ask you, did you know this kid who lived with Gregg?"

"I met him," Ricardo said, "and had dinner with him and Gregg once or twice."

"Do you know his name?" asked Dan.

"Uh huh, it's Luciano. He's from La Chorrera."

"Do you know his last name and his address?" Dan asked.

"No, but I know who does," Ricardo said. "The kid needed some dental work, so Gregg took him to that dentist behind the church that faces the park. You know, that dentist with the green hanging sign. I don't know the dentist's name, but he pulled one of Luciano's wisdom teeth and filled some cavities. He'd have a full name and maybe an address."

"Thanks man," Dan said. "Hang on here a minute. I'll be right back." Dan walked back to the group of police officers and talked with the oldest one there who Ricardo guessed was José Fernando. José Fernando then motioned for one of the other officers to come over, and Dan talked to the both of them. José Fernando said something to the other officer, and the other officer nodded and walked toward the front gate. Ricardo assumed he was off to talk to the dentist.

Dan came back to where Gregg was standing and brought José Fernando with him. After introductions, Dan said to Ricardo, "Puede usted decir a don José todo lo que sabe acerca de este muchacho?" asking Ricardo to tell José Fernando whatever he knew about Luciano. Ricardo had not realized that Dan spoke Spanish—it had never come up in his conversations before.

Ricardo told José Fernando all that he knew, starting with Gregg's description of befriending Luciano in the park and ending with the last conversation he had had with Gregg, where he learned that Gregg was planning to tell Luciano of his upcoming return to the States, meaning that Luciano would have to move out of Gregg's apartment.

José Fernando listened carefully, nodding his head, but Ricardo noticed that Dan was taking notes. Once a detective, always a detective, Ricardo thought, even if you're a disgruntled retired detective. When Ricardo finished, José Fernando leaned in and asked in almost a whisper if Gregg was gay. Ricardo nodded his head yes and said, "Creo que sí." Then José Fernando looked slightly uncomfortable and asked in the same low tone if Gregg and Luciano were intimate, meaning, were they lovers? Ricardo simply said, "No, nunca vi nada," indicating that he had never seen anything directly. Ricardo thought it best not to mention Alejandro's opinion of Gregg and Luciano's relationship for the moment.

José Fernando thanked Ricardo and Dan, and he left them to return to the group of police officers. Ricardo turned to Dan and asked, "What do you think?"

Dan just shrugged his shoulders and said, "Too early to tell."

Ricardo looked at Dan, and had the intuition that something was bothering Dan.

"But...?"

"Well," Dan said, "this was not a robbery. Gregg's wallet was on the table, and it still had money in it. But it was a violent crime. I counted almost twenty stab wounds, and they looked deep, which would indicate a crime of anger. I don't know. José Fernando said he would let me see the autopsy report...."

"But something else is bothering you?" Ricardo asked.

"Well, I wish the cops hadn't walked all over the apartment. Jesus Christ, they were stepping in the blood and leaving their own footprints... They didn't even have a camera to take crime scene photos for God's sake! I used my cell phone to take as many photos as I could. I'm going to see if I can get those printed up and look at them more closely."

Just then there was a commotion by Gregg's door. Ricardo looked over to see several of the younger officers carrying out Gregg's body on a stretcher. There was a bloody sheet over the body. As they navigated the stretcher through the apartment doorway, one arm fell out from under the sheet and dangled down.

"Fuck," said Dan. "What a circus." He went over to talk with José Fernando.

103

Ricardo watched them carry Gregg's body out and then walked back to other group just in time to hear Paul chastising Ted.

"I told you something like this would happen, Ted. You should have gotten rid of them weeks ago," Paul was saying.

"Shut up, Paul," Ted said.

Ricardo looked over at Carl. He seemed pale and shaky.

"You okay, Carl?" Ricardo asked.

"Yeah, no... I just didn't sign up for this," Carl said. "I just wanted to retire and live quietly. I wish I had gone with Jonathan this week."

"Well, that wouldn't be living quietly," Ted said.

But Ricardo was concerned. Carl did not look well. Ricardo suggested that they go sit at the table underneath the palm tree, and they all walked over there. Ricardo went into his apartment, unlocked the door, went inside and grabbed a bottle of water from the refrigerator. As he was about to walk out, he stopped and looked around, realizing that his apartment was right next door to a murder scene. It gave him the shivers. He walked outside, being careful to lock the apartment again, and went over to the patio table and gave the bottle of water to Carl.

"Here Carl, drink some water," he said.

"Thanks," Carl said and opened the bottle.

"Did you know him well?" Darren asked Ricardo as Ricardo sat down.

"No, not very well," Ricardo said. "He was a decent neighbor. Friendly, always willing to help."

Paul snorted, and said, "Well he helped himself, alright. That little gay boy slit his throat for all his help. Fucking little faggot got what he asked for, alright."

"No one deserves to die that way," Darren said.

"Well, he did!" said Paul. "Fucking queer, always prancing around and parading that boy in front of us."

Ted stood up and started shouting, "Fucking shit, Paul, I've had enough of you and your homophobic comments. I want you out of here by the end of the week! Just get your stuff and move the fuck out!"

Paul's face turned white. Then he stood up and started shouting at Ted something about having paid through the end of the month and having lived there for seven years. The police ran over and stood between them as Ted was shouting that he didn't care, that he'd give him his rent back but he had to be gone by the end of the week. Dan came over and shouted at both of them to shut up. Ted stormed off upstairs to his apartment and Paul likewise went into his apartment and slammed the door.

"Jesus Christ!" Carl said. "I gotta move out of here."

"Me too," said Darren.

Ricardo looked at Dan, and Dan just shook his head.

# Chapter 22: Splitting Apart

Paul didn't wait until the end of the week to move out. He did it the next day. Spent the morning packing his car in a frantic, haphazard way, with all the clothes and personal items from seven years of living there that he could cram into his car, and drove away. He made Carl go upstairs and get his rent back from Ted, which Ted later said he was glad to give to him to make him go away. He didn't say goodbye to anyone, and didn't leave a forwarding address, although everyone assumed he was moving to Panama City.

That afternoon after Paul had moved out, Ricardo was sitting in Dan's apartment listening to Dan tell him how the police had arrested Luciano.

"They found him at some apartment in La Chorrera, at the address he had given the dentist. Thank you for that, by the way. They arrested him without any incident. I was there when they questioned him."

Ricardo wondered how far Dan's friendship with José Fernando went, how it had started, and how he had such access. But he only asked, "And?"

"Well, the kid claimed that Gregg had loaned him his key, and had given him money to go buy some beer at that market downtown. He said he took longer than he should have because he stopped in the park to buy some marijuana. He claimed that when he got back, the door was open but the light was off. He said he went inside, stepped in something wet, turned on the light and saw that Gregg had been stabbed, panicked, and simply ran from the apartment. He said he knew he would be blamed."

"So he denies killing him?" Ricardo asked.

"Yeah... the cops were pretty rough on him, but he stuck to his story. By the way, did you see him or Gregg at all the day before yesterday?"

"No, I didn't see them that morning, and I was gone by mid-afternoon."

"Yeah, I heard about that," Dan chuckled. "Lucky for you. The police know Jenny. If she vouched for you, that's good enough for them."

"Why was that lucky for me?" Ricardo asked.

"Because Paul told the police you and Gregg were lovers." Dan said, and looked at Ricardo.

"What?! That's not true!" Ricardo said. "Why the fuck would he say that?"

"Well, he's kind of a kook, is what I think," Dan said.

Ricardo felt his anger rising. "That fucked-up motherfucker."

"Don't take it personally, buddy," Dan said. "After talking to Jenny, the police don't believe it at all. Like I said, Paul's kind of a kook. When was the last time you saw Gregg and this kid together?"

Ricardo was too angry to answer right away. He had never done anything to Paul except try to say hello. And yes, he did hang out with Gregg, but the fact that Paul would try to throw him under the bus for that was unfathomable. "Ah... shit... maybe two days ago? Yeah, I think I saw them going out to lunch at some time in the afternoon."

"Do you remember what the kid was wearing?" asked Dan.

"Well, I never saw him wear anything different than jeans, a black t-shirt and that thin hoodie. I don't think he kept a change of clothes here or anything."

"Yeah, that's what Darren saw him wearing the night Gregg was killed," said Dan.

"Darren?"

"Yeah, evidently Darren was the last one to see Gregg alive, sometime around nine that night. He said he stopped by to say hello to Gregg and saw that kid there, and that's what he was wearing. Jeans, a black t-shirt, and a light hoodie."

"Is that important?" Ricardo asked

"Well, that's what he was wearing when the police picked him up yesterday. And there was still dried blood on his feet, but you know what?"

"What?"

"No blood on his clothes," Dan said, and looked at Ricardo. "Not a drop."

Ricardo started to ask, "Could he have..."

"Changed clothes? Possibly, but the police searched the whole apartment where he was staying. He had other clothes there, but no blood. And there was no blood on his hands or arms. He could have washed that off, of course. But if he did, he forgot about the blood on his feet."

"Huh..." said Ricardo and thought about this for a minute.

"And you know what else?" Dan asked.

"What?"

"Next to Gregg's bed on the floor was a bag with a six-pack of beer along with a receipt with a time stamp that matched the time that the kid said he bought the beer."

"You think that Luciano's telling the truth?" Ricardo asked.

"Well, I wasn't ready to form an opinion until I looked at the photos on my cell phone. And even though those fuckhead cops had stepped in the blood, when I looked at the photos carefully, I realized there just weren't any bare feet footprints *except* those leaving the big pool of blood. Here, let me show you," said Dan reaching for his phone.

"No, no, that's okay," said Ricardo. "I'll take your word for it. So that means..."

"Well, it doesn't *mean* anything, but it certainly supports the kid's story, that he walked in, stepped in the pool of blood, turned on the light, and ran out. As many times as Gregg was stabbed, there should have been a lot bloody bare feet footprints inside that apartment—but there weren't. It doesn't mean he couldn't have done it or had an accomplice who did it. If the police hadn't fucked up the crime scene, I could have determined how many people were there. I asked José Fernando to collect all the shoes of the cops who were in the room that had any blood on them, so I could match them up to the photographs... if I can match them up."

Ricardo thought for a moment, and then asked, "So will the police let Luciano go?"

"Oh hell, no," said Dan. "They'll keep him in what they call 'preventive detention' until they decide whether to charge him or not."

"How long will that take?" asked Ricardo.

"Depends. Could take a few weeks or a few months. Could take a year," said Dan.

*　　*　　*

Carl was the next one to leave. He spent a few days moping around the Island, talking to anyone who'd listen about how horrible things had turned out for him. Even Darren got tired of listening to him complain. Ricardo thought Carl was hanging around in hopes that Jonathan would return. But Jonathan was evidently on an extended "fishing trip." Eventually, Carl booked a flight back to Ohio, saying the expat life was not for him. It was just as Dan had predicted. Carl didn't last two months. But even Dan couldn't have predicted the events that preceded Carl's departure.

That left only Darren and Ricardo living on the first floor. Gregg's apartment remained under police control for another week, and the police were daily visitors, going in and out of the apartment, talking to the residents, standing around, but not really accomplishing anything.

At some point that week, Ricardo threw the I Ching and got Hexagram 23, "Splitting Apart," indicating a time when "inferior people are pushing forward and about to crowd out the few remaining superior men". How apt, he thought. He read further. "It does not further one to go anywhere." Okay, he thought, I'll just hang out here until things get better... if they get better.

*     *     *

Darren was the next one to move out of the Island. He told Ricardo he was going to move in with some gringo woman who also volunteered at the community center. This came as news to Ricardo.

"Really?" Ricardo said. "Tell me about her. What's her name?"

"Her name is Barbara, and she's a retired school teacher from Florida. Just moved down here. Lives in La Chorrera but teaches English at the center. I met her about two weeks ago. She's very nice."

"Two weeks ago?" said Ricardo, "Isn't it kinda soon to move in together?"

"Oh no," explained Darren. "It's not like that. She has an extra room in the house that she rents in La Chorrera. I'm just subletting that room from her. It's strictly platonic."

"Uh huh, I see," said Ricardo. "But, you wouldn't be doing that if you didn't like her."

"Well yeah, sure," Darren sputtered. "She's very nice, very nice, but I'm not ready to get involved again. This is strictly platonic."

Ricardo laughed. "Dude, you are so ripe for the picking. Just let me know when the wedding is."

"No, no, no," Darren protested, "It's not like that."

"Whatever," Ricardo said.

*     *     *

That just left Ricardo as the only resident on the first floor. He considered moving somewhere else, but he decided to stay put. He told himself that, despite the murder, there still was not another complex in Villa Rosario that had the features that the Island had, and that the murder was not a reflection on the Island's security but just a fluke, but mostly he stayed because he felt, like the Hexagram said, it simply did not further him to go anywhere.

Eventually, the police removed all the police tape from in front of Gregg's apartment. Ted hired a cleaning service to come in and bleach the entire apartment and have it completely repainted. But Ted couldn't rent any of the apartments out. Everyone knew there had been a murder there.

One day, Ricardo was surprised to see the police come back. They hadn't been there for several days and Ricardo had assumed that they were done with their investigation. But they came back and went into Paul's apartment and started hauling things out. Ricardo watched them for a bit and then went upstairs to ask Dan about it.

"Hey Dan, do you know what's going on downstairs?" Ricardo asked through the screen door.

"Oh hey Ricardo, come on in," said Dan. "Yeah, actually I do. They're searching Paul's apartment."

"Why?"

"Well, a couple of reasons. First, the police decided not to charge that Luciano kid. Well, they charged him with buying the marijuana that he confessed to, which they found in his pocket when they arrested him. But he's off the hook for the murder rap."

"Really?" said Ricardo. "So they released him?"

"Uh huh, everything he said matched up. The clerk at the store remembered him buying the beer. And I showed José Fernando the photos I took of the bloody floor and explained how it would have been impossible for the kid to have stabbed Gregg so many times, so violently, without moving his feet. The footprints were that kid's best alibi. That and the fact that there was no blood anywhere on him except the soles of his feet."

"So why are they searching Paul's apartment?" Ricardo asked.

"Routine," Dan explained. "They should have done it

the day he moved out. I don't know why they didn't, but once they let the kid go, Paul became their next best suspect because of the things he said about Gregg. He obviously hated Gregg."

"Obviously," said Ricardo.

"Well, it's a long shot, but you never know. Like I say, they should have searched everyone's apartment the day of the crime, but Panama justice works differently. By the way, I got the autopsy report back today. Want to see it?"

"Nooo," Ricardo said.

"Ha, pussy," Dan said. "Well, it's interesting. Basically it said that Gregg died because his throat was slit, not because of the stab wounds."

"Huh," said Ricardo, "that's what Paul said."

Dan looked at Ricardo hard.

"What?!"

"Yeah," said Ricardo. "That's what started the fight between Paul and Ted at the table that day. Paul claimed that Luciano slit Gregg's throat."

"Really? Do you remember the exact quote?"

"Um well, we were all talking about Gregg, and um, Darren said that no one deserved to get killed like that, and I said something about Gregg always being friendly or helpful or something, and then Paul said that Luciano, well, to be exact, he said 'that little gay boy slit his throat for being so friendly' or something like that."

"Wow," said Dan. "That's interesting... because with all the blood, none of us knew that Gregg's throat had been cut until we got the autopsy report."

"Oh..." was all Ricardo could say.

The two men sat in silence for the next few minutes.

Finally Dan stood up and said, "If you'll excuse me, I'm going to go downstairs and see how the search is going."

"Yeah sure," Ricardo said. "I've got some stuff to do myself."

114

# Chapter 23: Time to Come Home?

Ricardo had deliberately put off emailing Alison with news of Gregg's murder, but after leaving Dan's apartment, he thought he was ready to write her. He knew that as soon as he told her what had happened, she would barrage him with concerns. On one hand, he liked that she cared about him, but on the other hand, he was anticipating that she would start pestering him to come back to the States. And he was right. He sent her a lengthy but carefully-worded email describing what had happened, how Ted had found Gregg's body, how the police had arrested Luciano but then released him, and how the investigation had shifted focus to Paul. He was careful to stress that Paul was gone from the Island and could not get back in (he didn't want her worrying about his safety), and he was careful to omit any reference to his alibi. Within ten minutes of hitting the email send button, he started getting a flurry of short emails back, starting with *What!!!* and continuing one after the other with questions or concerns. He tried to respond to each one as fast as he could, but they just kept coming. Finally he wrote: "Look, there's nothing to worry about. Let's Skype tonight around eight your time, okay?" She wrote back, "No, let's Skype now!" Ricardo sighed, and typed: "Okay, give me ten minutes, and I'll call you."

He used the ten minutes to go to the bathroom, and brew a fresh pot of coffee, and get some crackers to nibble on. He was anticipating a long Skype session. And he was right about that too.

First she wanted to know in detail everything that

had happened, but Ricardo didn't want to risk her asking where he was when the murder happened, so he decided to block any such recounting.

"Look," he said, "I've already emailed you the whole story. There's nothing more to say. Nobody saw it happen. Nobody knows when it happened. Nobody heard anything. Carl was up real early and saw blood and he and Ted called the police. End of story."

"Why didn't you tell me all this earlier?" she demanded.

"Well," he answered, "A, because I didn't want to worry you. B, because at first it looked like an open and shut case, and C, I did write you as soon as it was clear that they suspected Paul was the murderer."

"Oh, Ricardo!" she said. "I hate this. Wasn't he next door to you? It could have been you. Was your door locked? You didn't hear anything? Do you think that Paul guy really did this? What if he comes back?"

"Alison, slow down. Everything's okay. I told you no one heard anything, and my door is always locked. Yes, it does seem that Paul did it, but he's gone. He can't get back in. He doesn't have a key anymore."

"He could have had a copy made," she said.

"Alison, if he did kill Gregg, he's not going to come back. If he didn't kill Gregg, he's still not coming back because Ted told him to keep away."

"Well, if he didn't kill Gregg, who did?" she asked.

"I don't have an answer to that, but I might in a day or two. The police hauled away a couple of boxes of stuff from Paul's apartment. Dan says they'll send it to some lab in Panama City. If there's evidence there that incriminates Paul, well, I guess they'll arrest Paul. But in any case, I'm safe. You know me, Alison. If I didn't feel safe, I would leave. But hell, I'm probably safer her than I would be in Panama City, where I might run into Paul."

Alison was quiet for a second and then she said, "Look, Ricardo, why don't you come up here for two to three weeks? The weather's okay now, and I would feel better."

Ricardo pursed his lips, then said, "Thank you sweetie, that's a nice offer. But I'm going to wait a bit. Let me talk to Dan some more and see how this thing unfolds. I promise you, if I in any way feel unsafe, I will hop a plane out of here."

"Ricardo, you know I love you."

"I love you too, Alison, but let's just wait a bit. Just a few more days, and we can talk again and revisit this issue."

Ricardo thought he could hear her crying just a bit, but he didn't want to ask. Finally she said, "Okay... but if anything happens to you, I'll never forgive myself for not making you come home now."

Ricardo ignored the fact that she was using the word *home* to apply to both of them, and instead said, "I promise you baby, everything is going to be alright. Now, let's talk about something different. How's your painting doing?"

"Ricardo, how can I paint now?"

"See?" Ricardo said, "I knew I shouldn't have told you at all. This is going to interfere with your art. I can tell you that none of this has interfered with my writing."

Actually, Ricardo was lying about this—he hadn't written anything since Gregg's murder. But he didn't want Alison to know that.

"If I can write, you can paint, okay?" he said.

"Okay," she said. "I miss you."

"I miss you too, baby."

They talked for about thirty more minutes. Alison would try to steer the conversation back to Gregg's murder and how she was worried for Ricardo, but Ricardo kept insisting he was okay. He promised to consider her invitation for a short "vacation" at her house.

"Ha," he said, "a vacation from my vacation."

"You know what I mean," she said. "Let's just call it a safe-cation."

"Ha, that's funny, a safe-cation. Look, I promise you,

I will think about it. Let's talk again in about three days, okay? I'll text before I call. Okay?"

"Okay."

*　　*　　*

And Ricardo did think seriously about it, not because he felt that his personal safety was in jeopardy, but because he missed Alison. He weighed the options, made mental pro/con lists, and tried to visualize what it would mean to their relationship if he did go spend a few weeks with her. But a few weeks this soon after her last visit would move their relationship a notch closer to something permanent. As much as he missed her, he could not bring himself to look at airline flight schedules. He did love Alison, but he had loved Eve, and he had loved Haley before that, and two wives before that, plus other women and other men. He knew those relationships failed partly because he had spent too much time with them, too much time loving them and living with them. Whether he was simply selfish, or had a hypersensitive need for time alone, he didn't know. One therapist years ago had told him he was afraid of commitment. That, of course, was not helpful. He didn't want to lose Alison, and on some level he knew he would lose her if he went to stay with her this soon. If he could wait until their rendezvous in December, he thought their relationship would endure.

He cursed Miguel again for using the word *novia* to describe Alison. *Novia* means both fiancée or girlfriend in Spanish, depending on the context. He was willing to accept Alison as his novia, but only in the girlfriend sense of the word.

# Chapter 24:   Warrant

Two days after his Skype session with Alison, Dan came knocking at Ricardo's door.

"Hey, come on in, Dan," Ricardo said. "What's up?"

"Well, I thought you'd like to know. Guess what they found in Paul's apartment?" Dan asked.

"A bloody knife?" Ricardo asked.

"No, ha, I wish, that would have cinched it. No, but they did find bleach and bloody rags. I think if the police hadn't trampled on Gregg's floor and front steps, I could have found traces of bleach and some blood smears there. As it was, they found a couple of blood spots on Paul's front steps and inside his apartment. José Fernando sent them to the lab to see if they match Gregg's blood, but I'm sure they will. So is José. He got a warrant issued for Paul's arrest this morning."

"Well, that's good," said Ricardo.

"Yeah, well, it would be if we knew where he was, but we don't."

"Did you talk to Ted?"

"He doesn't know where Paul moved to, either," Dan said.

"No, I mean about Paul's hang-outs in Panama City. Before they stopped being friends, they used to go there together."

"Oh that. Yeah, I know," Dan said. "Ted gave us the name of some brothel and a couple of strip-joints, but I'm not holding my breath."

"Why not?" asked Ricardo. "It's a small country. If

he hasn't crossed a border, then isn't it just a matter of time before you find him? I mean, gringos stand out down here."

"Yeah, well, we thought so too. But when we contacted the U.S. Embassy, they didn't have any record of anyone here under his name, and we tried all different spelling variations."

"Really?"

"Yeah, so I thought, well maybe's he's not a U.S. citizen. But we tried all the other embassies. Nothing. Which means he has no passport. It never dawned on me," Dan said, "until I talked to the Embassy. But he was here for seven years."

"Yeah... and?"

"Well, according to Ted, Paul never left the country. Never left the country. Doesn't that strike you as odd?" Dan asked.

"Well..." Ricardo said and then paused, "Oh... he'd have to have residency. Otherwise, he'd have to leave every ninety days."

"Right!" Dan said, "but he wasn't a resident. José Fernando checked it out carefully. He was here illegally, which means.... we don't know who he is."

"Wow."

"Uh huh," Dan continued. "Wow is right. Seven years and we don't have a name or a photo. I wrote up a description of what he looked like, and José Fernando has sent it to all the airports, ports, and borders. But I have a hunch he's good at hiding. Did you ever notice that he shaved his head?"

"Uh, of course, how could you not notice?"

"Sorry, that was a stupid question. What I meant was, did you ever notice that he wasn't bald?"

"What do you mean?" Ricardo asked.

"Well I noticed it one time but never thought anything about it. Most guys who shave their heads do so because they're bald or going bald, or occasionally, they have a head that just looks good shaved. But Paul wasn't going bald. I noticed it one evening when he was standing under the porch light. Yet he shaved his head every single morning. Shaved it close. Seven years. And he was not the kind of guy who looked better with a shaved head."

"So, you think it was a deliberate disguise?" Ricardo asked.

"Uh huh, I do." said Dan. "I'm hoping that the description that José Fernando sent out will bring back a wanted poster from somewhere, something with a photo and a name."

"Wow," Ricardo said again.

"And here's something else," Dan said. "We checked all the local banks, here and in La Chorrera. No one fitting his description had a Panamanian bank account. That means that the only way he could be getting money would be to use an ATM card and pull cash out each week. José Fernando has his guys interviewing all the guards and tellers at all the local banks. But so far no one can say they ever saw him at an ATM. But we're checking the security cameras. Hopefully, there will be a photo of him."

"What do you think the chances are of him coming back here?" Ricardo asked.

"Here? Probably nil, but I would tell your little manager friend down at the supermarket to be careful, just in case. I mean, it's clear that Paul had some hatred of gays."

Ricardo felt his back stiffen up. How did Dan know about Alejandro? He looked at Dan without saying anything.

As if Dan was reading Ricardo's thoughts, he said, "Well, I got eyes, dude. Everyone knows that guy is gay, and I saw him over here a few times with you. I'm just saying, don't tell him about the whole investigation, but fill him in on what he needs to know to be alert, that's all."

Ricardo thought for a second more, then nodded his head and said. "I will." Then he decided to change the subject. "So, how does it feel to be back in the detective business?"

Dan took a breath. "Well, I was good at it. Those guys back home lost a good detective."

"I can testify to that," Ricardo said.

"Well, the good news is that José Fernando is very happy. He's got good evidence, a warrant out, so his work is done. And the best thing, from his point of view, is that the suspect is not a Panamanian, but another gringo. They don't like it down here when locals kill gringos—it's bad for the tourist business. But if a gringo kills a gringo, hey, it's business as usual. Yup, José is happy, and if José is happy, then Berghoff's is happy, and if Berghoff's is happy, then I'm happy."

"There's probably more there than I want to know," Ricardo said.

"Probably," Dan said. "You want to grab some beers later on?"

"Sure."

# Chapter 25: Like Rats

Albert was the next one to leave the Island. It was about a month after Gregg's murder that Ted called an ambulance when he found Albert incoherent while checking on him. The ambulance took Albert to a private hospital in Panama City, but he only got worse. He died two days later.

Ricardo and Dan helped Ted box up Albert's belongings.

"I've been in touch with his son in Alaska," explained Ted. "He doesn't want us to throw anything away. He says he'll pay the shipping costs to send everything to him."

Ted was more torn up about Albert's death than he was about Gregg's.

"I've known Albert for ten years," he said when he asked Dan and Ricardo for their help. "He was a good guy. I just don't think I can do this task alone. He was the longest tenant here. Never bothered anyone. He would take long walks with binoculars to watch for birds. Before he got sick, he and I would sit out here on the balcony and drink whiskey at night and talk politics. We never agreed on anything, but I loved our discussions."

Both Dan and Ricardo agreed to help, of course. They even volunteered to do it for Ted, but Ted said no, he wanted to be there. They ended up filling eight boxes with Albert's possessions. Three of the boxes were just old clothes, and the other five boxes contained a decade's worth of personal belongings, the meaning of which, like most people's prized possessions, was indecipherable. But the three men wrapped each item carefully in newspaper and placed them in the boxes. Ricardo found a small Asian ceramic bowl in a

Ziploc bag, and inside the bowl was an artificial flower, some prayer beads, a dried water chestnut, a small cameo stone from a ring and a brass pixie charm for a necklace. Clearly, each of these items held some important memory for Albert, and Ricardo tried to imagine what each would be. Perhaps the flower came from the hair of some girl, or the cameo stone from a deceased relative, or perhaps the brass pixie was a childhood good luck charm. But whatever the true history was, like most meaning, it died when Albert died. Perhaps Albert's son might remember what some of them meant, and perhaps that might bring him comfort. Ricardo hoped so.

\*         \*         \*

Jonathan was the next one to leave the Island. He returned from Sosua about a week before Albert died. He listened quietly to the news of Gregg's death. The next day, he said he was going back to Sosua to think about all this. Maybe he realized that his entire audience was gone, or maybe he didn't like the real world intruding on his satyristic paradise. Maybe he was just scared. He returned to the Island about two weeks later, and when he heard that Albert had died, he simply said, "That's it." He moved out a few days later. Ted said that he had moved to some adults-only apartment complex in Panama City and that Jonathan claimed he did it because it was more convenient to be closer to the airport for his frequent travels.

Ricardo took advantage of Jonathan's departure to move upstairs to Jonathan's old apartment. He didn't like being the only one on the first floor, and it still creeped him out to be stuck between Paul's old apartment and Gregg's old apartment. Plus, he liked having Dan as a next door neighbor to talk with.

That left Ted, Dan, and Ricardo as the only remaining residents in the Island. Louis, of course, was still paying rent on the apartment upstairs next to where Ricardo was now living, but Louis hadn't been to the Island in six months. And Ricardo still had never met him. Ted said that he thought

Louis would show up in about another month to stay a week or two.

Dan kept Ricardo up to date on the search for Paul. They would usually sit on the balcony patio in the evening, watch the sunset, and drink. Ted would often join them.

"Well, it's not exactly a search," Dan was explaining to the two of them one night. "I mean, there's no posse or special team out searching for him. But the warrant is out. If some cop stumbles across him, they'll arrest him. At least now we have a grainy photograph."

The photograph was from an ATM camera, showing Paul taking money out of the machine in Villa Rosario. It wasn't a great photograph, but it captured his bitter scowl. The flyer also had an artist's sketch, based on Dan's description, showing both a bald-headed face and a sketch of how Paul would look if his hair grew back.

"What about the ATM card?" Ricardo asked Dan. "Wasn't there a name on that?"

"No," said Dan, "actually there wasn't. It was a corporate ATM card, some innocuous name out of the Bahamas. Berghoff's has an office there, so I'm having them check it out, but I suspect it's just a fake address. If this was the states, we could get a warrant. And the next time he used that card at any bank, we'd know where he was instantly. But they just don't have the technology or the law enforcement sophistication for that down here. José Fernando is having his men visit different banks in Panama City, one by one, to look through their records to see if that card has been used recently. But it's a daunting process, like finding a needle in a haystack. Besides, my hunch is that he crossed the border into either Costa Rica or Columbia. Both borders are pretty porous."

"You know," Ricardo said, "Gregg told me once that he thought Paul had been a big honcho in the surfing world. I wonder if any old surfing magazine would have some mention of him, some article with his real name."

"Yeah," Dan said, "I've got a friend back in L.A. looking into that. Nothing yet so far."

"Maybe he has a fake passport," Ted suggested, "and he caught a plane out of the country using that."

"Well, that's actually hard to do these days," Dan said. "Ever since 9/11, the one area where technology has improved is with passports. Almost all of them have bar codes now, and they get scanned at the airport. The U.S. keeps huge data banks on who's going where, whether they're U.S. citizens or not."

"Can they do that?" Ricardo asked. "Keep track of where foreigners go?"

"Absolutely," said Dan. "Even if it weren't legal, they would do it anyway. So there's that, plus we sent his wanted poster to all the Panamanian seaports and land border crossings. No, if he was going to leave the country, he would do it through the jungle, but that's easy to do. Undocumented workers travel back and forth through Panama all the time. My guess is that he'd head to Colombia. Costa Rica would be too dangerous for him."

"How so?" Ted asked.

"Because Costa Rica's got one of the better police forces in Central America. He'd be more likely to be caught there. Colombian police would only care about a warrant for a gringo because they know they would get a bigger bribe off a gringo to let him go."

"I wonder if they'll ever catch him," Ricardo said.

"Oh, eventually," said Dan. "Eventually, they always get caught. Some rookie cop will stumble upon his trail, or he'll run low on money, or enough time will go by and he'll get careless and cross the wrong border. I helped José Fernando prepare a complete case file with all the evidence, so even if it's five or six years down the road, Panama will still be able to prosecute him easily."

"Five or six years..." said Ricardo. "Wow."

"Not to change the subject, fellas," interjected Ted, "but speaking of money, I've got to rent some of these units out. I've never had so many vacancies here before. If either of you two have any friends who are thinking of moving to, or even visiting Panama, can you tell them about this place?

I'll make it worth your while. I'm getting no inquiries at all."

"Well, if you'd stop letting so many people die here, it would help," said Dan.

"That's not funny," said Ted. "I mean it, the government taxes me based on the square footage of the building, not on whether it's occupied or not, and the taxes here are huge. I'm losing money on this building if I can't rent some apartments out."

"Why don't you rent to some of the locals?" suggested Ricardo.

"Well, I might have to do that," said Dan. "I used to think gringos were less trouble, but now I'm not sure. The trouble with renting to locals is you rent to one guy and suddenly there's a whole family living there, with a grandmother and three kids. I like a quiet place."

"It's pretty quiet now," teased Dan.

"Yeah, I know," said Ted. "I'm going to give it another month. If I can't rent some units out, I may have to open it up to locals."

Ricardo kept his opinions about Ted's racism to himself, but he would have preferred having more people here too. It was too quiet now. More like a morgue. The "Morgue of Misfits", he thought to himself.

## Chapter 26:   A Woman's Intuition

Alison kept worrying about Ricardo ever since he had told her about Gregg's murder. If he didn't call her to chat once a week, she would call him. This was a new behavior for her. Ricardo was used to being the one who always initiated contact with her. At first he was flattered. But as the weeks went by, it began to irritate him. He kept hoping that, as more time went by, she would relax a bit and not worry about his safety so much. But she continued to press him to come to Santa Fe. He continued to put her off, saying he would come in December.

"Call it a woman's intuition, Ricardo," she said one day on Skype, "but I just think you ought to come up here for a couple of weeks. If you don't want to stay at my place, I can find somewhere for you to stay."

"Ah, yeah... well, first of all, Alison, if I'm gonna travel to Santa Fe, I'm gonna stay with you, in your bed, not at some friend's house. But second of all, the timing just isn't good right now. I'm perfectly safe here. Nothing bad's going to happen to me. And I'm getting some good writing done lately, and I don't want to interrupt that."

That part was true. Ricardo had started writing again. After he moved upstairs, away from Gregg's and Paul's old apartments, he felt more relaxed. He liked the view from the second floor better. He arranged the writing table so that it allowed him to look out over the whole valley. It seemed to inspire him. Which was good because, right on schedule, his publisher had started emailing him, asking him—gently—if he was writing, and Ricardo was able to tell him truthfully that he was. Over the years, his publisher had published Ricardo's poems, his short stories and his novels. But he preferred publishing the novels because, as he bluntly admitted, he could charge more for them and make more money off them. Ricardo had stopped working on that little exercise that Alison had originally suggested, writing about the men at the Island. After Gregg's murder, Ricardo just couldn't work on those descriptions anymore. He put that writing aside, hoping that maybe one day he might return to it. In the meantime, since he moved upstairs, he had started working on a series of poems and short stories that were more political than his usual work. Ever since he had started thinking about all his conversations with Alison about the politics of prostitution, he had been turning an idea over in his head about how the financial position of men shaped their relationships with women—especially with prostitutes—and how the women compensated for the power differential through charm, guile, lying, and good business sense. He had gone back to Jenny's several times. Not only for the sex, but just to talk to Jenny. At first she was reluctant when he told her he wanted to interview her. So he had Miguel talk with her, and they both reassured her that Ricardo only wanted to interview her for background material. It wasn't all work, however. On those evenings when Magali was available, Ricardo would extend his visit an extra few hours just to have sex with her. On other occasions, he also would join Miguel and Alejandro at the bathhouse. He felt like he was producing some good poems and short stories. Life seemed to be returning to a normal rhythm of sex and writing, and Ricardo didn't want to leave either one.

"You can write here," Alison said. "I can set up a desk for you when I'm in the studio. You'll have privacy and space."

"I appreciate that, baby," Ricardo said. "But I'm on a roll here. If I get to a natural break in the writing, I'll think about coming up. But right now I can't."

After each conversation with Alison, Ricardo felt sad. This was how it always started, the small thin crack that eventually fractured the relationship. A woman always wanted something that Ricardo didn't want, and either directly or indirectly, and she wouldn't take no for an answer. At least Alison was direct about it, so Ricardo wasn't left guessing what she wanted. But still, there was that impasse.

Ricardo was talking to Miguel about it one day in the bathhouse.

"I just don't understand why she just won't do her thing, let me do mine, and we get together when we do. If it's good when we're together, if it's meant to be, then it'll grow naturally," Ricardo was saying.

"Ah, my friend," said Miguel. "You want the impossible. You want a woman to treat you like a man. They cannot do that. It is not in their nature... How do you gringos say it? They are not programmed for it. Ha, you want them to be like little computers. They will never treat you like an equal. And do you know why?"

"Why?"

"Because you are not equals."

"Oh yeah? Who do you think is superior?" Ricardo asked.

"No, no, I do not mean either one is better," Miguel explained. "That's the problem with men—they want to make it a competition. What I am saying is simply that there is no equality between men and women. My father once told me when I was a child that men are like dogs and women are like cats. I think he was right. It was just my fate that I prefer dogs."

"Well, shit, Miguel, I like both dogs and cats... but I do like this particular cat. If she'd just stop being such a pest."

"She won't. She can't help it. The day she stops asking you to visit her is the day you will lose her, my friend."

*   *   *

It was about two weeks after Ricardo's conversation with Miguel in the bathhouse that Ricardo was sitting in a small café in Villa Rosario. He had bought a paper across the street and had taken to the café to read over a cup of coffee and a pastry. The front page carried the usual news of drinking water problems and political corruption. But in the inside crime section, he found a small article about a homeless boy being found stabbed to death down by the river on the outskirts of La Chorrera. The article provided very little detail, and the victim was not identified. Normally, the death of a homeless person would not have made the papers. But this was a stabbing, and that's what caught Ricardo's eye. The article implied that the body had been stabbed multiple times. Ricardo had a bad feeling in his stomach. He asked the waitress for a bag to take the rest of his pastry home, paid the cashier, and walked back to the Island. There he knocked on Dan's door, but no one answered.

Late that afternoon, he heard someone's steps coming up the landing. Ricardo stepped out on the patio and saw Dan.

"Hey, Dan," he started to say. "Did you see the..."

But Dan completed his sentence. "The article about that kid getting knifed in La Chorrera? Yeah, that's where I've been all afternoon. And I know your next question. And yes, it was Gregg's boy. Same pattern of knife wounds."

Dan looked worried. Ricardo did not like that.

"Do you think..."

"The answer to that question is also yes. I think it's likely Paul. Hang on a second, Ricardo. I need to pee. I'll be right back." Dan unlocked his door and went into his apartment. Ricardo sat down on the patio chair and waited for him to return. Shit, he thought. This changes things. He tried to think it through, but his thoughts were racing too fast. Paul would not have known where Luciano lived, so he would have had to hang around La Chorrera hoping to stop him. But how would he even know the kid lived in La Chorrera? Did he overhear Gregg talking? Did Gregg

132

ever talk to Paul? Gregg talked to everyone, and it would have been the kind of thing Gregg would say. He was such a blabbermouth. But bottom line, it meant that Paul was still nearby.

He heard the toilet flush, and in a minute Dan reappeared and took a seat on the patio.

"I feel better now," he said. "Yeah, it was that kid. I got the call from José Fernando this morning. I had to call Berghoff's and tell them I couldn't come in, and they understood. But listen, Ricardo, this is serious. I knew when I saw the number of stab wounds in Gregg's body that we had a nutcase on our hands, but I had ascribed a bit of logic and common sense to Paul once I learned that he had been living under the radar for seven years. I figured he would be smart enough to leave the country, head to Colombia. And the fact that this kid... what was his name? Luciano? The fact that this Luciano kid got stabbed the same way could be a fluke, a pure coincidence. But in my twenty years as a detective, I never saw a coincidence. Every time some perp claimed it was just a coincidence, it turned out to be totally premeditated. My point is, that assuming Paul did this, well you've already figured it out. It means he's still around. It means that he's much more dangerous than we've given him credit for. Shit... what I'm trying to say, Ricardo, is that maybe you might want to think about getting out of Panama for a while. I'm not saying you're on any kind of hit list or anything. But this Luciano murder puts a whole new twist on things. If Paul saw you hanging out with Gregg, or saw that gay store manager friend of yours over here, he might be just crazy enough to target you. Hell, for all we know, he could have some paranoid vendetta against everyone who lived here at this apartment complex. He could think that his getting thrown out of here was some type of conspiracy. Now, José Fernando has got all his guys on alert both here and in La Chorrera, but you know the police force down here. They're not well-trained. Well, hell, they're not trained at all. If Paul was a usual idiot criminal, they could catch him, but he's been very successful at changing his identity and keeping under the radar. Anyway, you get my point... you might want to think about a little vacation."

"Hmm. Shit, Dan, I don't know what to think. You really think it was Paul?" Ricardo asked.

"Well, the kid's throat was cut first, just like Gregg's. We knew that from the amount of blood. Paul cuts the throat first, and then he starts stabbing them. Mostly in the back. But there's little blood from the back wounds. Most likely both guys were already dead when Paul started stabbing them. It has all the marks of a ritualistic psychopathic killing. The kid also had a little bit of money on him, and the killer didn't take that. We did get some photos of some shoe prints this time. That might end up being good evidence. But first we need to catch him... But, to answer your question, yes, I really think it was Paul."

"Okay... shit, okay, well, thanks, Dan," Ricardo said, and went inside his apartment.

He sat down at his desk and just thought for a minute. Then he opened up his laptop and emailed Alison.

It took him several drafts to get the wording just right. He didn't want to alarm her. He didn't want to tell her about Luciano. He didn't know how long he might need to be out of Panama. Finally, he settled on the message: "If your offer is still open, I'd like to take you up on it and come visit you. Can you put up with me for a week or two?"

Then he went out on the patio and walked over to Ted's apartment. Dan was already inside, telling Ted what had happened. Ted looked grim as he listened to Dan.

Ted looked up at Ricardo and said, "You gonna move out?"

"Not exactly, Ted," Ricardo said. "I like this place. But I'm going to take a little vacation. I'm going to leave my stuff here, and I'll pay you in advance for next month's rent. I want to come back here. But for the moment, I think I'll get out of town for awhile."

"Well," Ted said, "I don't blame you. Dan wants me to do the same thing, but I can't."

Dan said, "I understand, Ted. Tell you what, I'll ask

José Fernando to have a cop car drive by regularly. If he has an extra car, maybe he'll agree to park it here. There won't be a cop inside it, but it may give the appearance of a police presence."

Ricardo had a thought. "You know, Dan, there are lots of empty apartments here. Maybe José Fernando has got some young officers who'd like to live there rent free for a month or two, or three."

Dan looked at Ted. Ted grimaced, but nodded his head. "Yeah, I'd be willing to do that. Fuck, I'm not renting them out anyway."

"That's a good idea, Ricardo. I'll ask José Fernando."

\* \* \*

Alison's email reply was waiting when Ricardo got back to his apartment. "Absolutely! Let me know your flight info, and I'll pick you up!"

He typed back. "Thanks. I'll probably be there tomorrow night. I'm going to make the reservations now and will email you as soon as I have an arrival time."

Alison emailed back. "Wow! Is everything okay?"

"Yeah, I'm okay," he typed back. "Sorry for the short notice. I'll explain when I get there. Give me a few minutes to look for tickets."

Ricardo started checking the different airlines, wincing at how much flying out the next day was going to cost him. If he waited two weeks, he could save $400, but he knew he wasn't going to do that. Finally, he gave up looking at prices, and simply booked a flight that had the best schedule.

As he typed in his credit card number, he thought to himself: "Running from a killer, $1200. Saving your life... Priceless."

# Chapter 27: Returning to the States

Over the past six years, Ricardo had flown back and forth from Panama to the United States numerous times, and each time he hated it more and more. He used to enjoy flying, seeing all the different types of travelers, talking to them, finding out where they were going to or coming from, getting a little sample of their lives and aspirations. But it seemed to him the past few years that the interesting adventuresome idealistic travelers had all somehow disappeared and had been replaced by fat, self-satisfied, rich arrogant travelers. Talking to them always left Ricardo feeling drained and annoyed, so he had stopped trying to engage with them. He figured that the young adventuresome types must have given up on Central America, and were off exploring more remote countries in Asia, leaving Panama to wealthy ex-pats and real estate agents.

He flew from Panama City to Dallas, sat around in the Dallas airport for two hours, then caught a plane to Santa Fe. By the time he got to the Santa Fe airport, it was dark and he was exhausted. Alison, to her credit, was like her old self, sweet and understanding and not putting any pressure on him.

"Listen, baby," he explained when she picked him up at the airport. "Can you do me a big favor and just let me chill out tonight, drink some wine, get some decent food, and drink some more wine? Tomorrow, I promise I will answer any questions you have, but tonight I'm cranky and tired and I just want to zone out. It's been a long day."

"Of course, Ricardo," she said. "I'm just glad to have

you here. I've got two bottles of Sauvignon Blanc chilling in the fridge, and I also have some leftover lasagna I can heat up, or we can stop and pick up something."

"Lasagna sounds fine, baby. It's good to see you, too. It's real good to see you."

The next day, of course, over morning coffee, he did have to explain everything. Alison asked a few questions, but mostly just listened. When Ricardo was out of words, they both just sat there quietly. She reached over and took his hand.

"I'm just glad you're okay," she said.

"Me too."

"Do you have any plans?"

"Well," Ricardo said, "that's a good question. Actually, no. This whole thing happened so fast. I mean, basically Dan said 'go' and I went. I paid Ted rent for next month, but I'm not sure what has to happen before I feel safe to go back."

Alison squeezed his hand but didn't say anything.

"I haven't even told my publisher I'm back in the States," Ricardo said. "I'm sure he'd love to arrange some readings or something for me."

"Well Ricardo, maybe it would be good to just do nothing for a couple of days, don't try and make any decisions. If you need a space for writing, there's a desk in the upstairs meditation room. I've got the paintings I'm currently working on and I won't bother you."

"Thank you, baby. You're a lifesaver," Ricardo said.

*       *       *

That afternoon Ricardo set up his laptop at the desk in Alison's meditation room. He emailed his publisher in New York saying that he was back in the States for a few weeks, explained his recent interviews with Jenny and his thoughts on a new book, asked for an update on sales in Europe and the U.S. on his last books, but didn't offer to do any publicity or book signings. He liked Alison's advice about not doing anything. Besides, he didn't feel much like writing. He scanned over his notes from the interviews with Jenny, but they didn't hold any interest for him.

He started thinking about the murders. Where did Paul go between Gregg's murder and Luciano's murder? How did he survive? Did he change his appearance? Where was he getting money? He wondered what progress Dan and José Fernando were making. He emailed Dan to let him know he had arrived in the states safely and asked him to keep him posted on any developments in the case. He thought about Dan's comments on the quality of the Panama police force and wondered if they would ever catch Paul. If the guy was so good at living under the radar for seven years, what chance would they have of finding him? And *why* was he living under the radar? The more Ricardo thought about it, the more it made sense that no one does that unless they are hiding from something, and that something would probably be a crime, which means there would be a warrant for him with a photo and fingerprints. But Dan didn't have any fingerprints to send to the FBI to look for old warrants, which meant that someone would have to look through old warrant mugshots one by one, looking for a young Paul. And the only people who really knew what Paul looked liked were in Panama, and none of them were pouring over mug shots. And Paul could be from any state, so there would literally be millions of old warrant photos to go through. But what about the surfer angle? Ricardo thought. If he was really an old surfer, he would almost have to have been living in California during his younger years. And if he was any good, he would have entered surfing competitions. And if he had won any of them, there might be photographs in old surfing magazine. Dan had said that he had a friend back in L.A. looking into that, but "looking into that" would mean, like the mugshot search, looking thorough old magazines or newspapers for a photograph of a young surfer. Some of those old magazines might not even be on the internet— they might be on microfiche, or more likely in boxes in someone's attic. And even if Dan did have a friend willing to dedicate the time to looking for and through old surfing archives, that friend would only have the ATM photo of Paul to reference.

Ricardo figured that the Santa Fe public library wouldn't have any copies of old surfing magazines. And he also figured that using the internet to search for old surfing pictures of Paul was a total waste of time. But...he had time to waste, and he somehow felt that he had to be doing something about Paul if he could. Ricardo hadn't been a big fan of Gregg or Luciano. But no act of mutual sexual exploitation made Paul's actions comprehensible to Ricardo. Besides, Ricardo didn't feel safe returning to Villa Rosario as long as there was a possibility that Paul might be lurking around there.

So, Ricardo spent that afternoon on the internet, throwing out random searches on Google using variations of phrases that combined "surfing" with "competition", "California", "championship", etc., starting with the year 1963, and moving on up. He quickly learned that most of the still-active surfing magazines kept archives of their old issues, but that those old copies were collector items, each often selling for more than a hundred dollars. Only their covers were available on the internet. However, he still was able to find a fair number of articles available that were not connected to rare issues. But if they had close-up photos of the faces of the then-current surfers, he saw how similar all the young faces looked: white, smiling, blonde hair, and oh so young. He realized he had never seen Paul smile, so he had no idea what he would look like smiling. And that was assuming the old articles had photos to look at. Many articles didn't come with photos. He hadn't realized how much change had happened in the world of media with the advent of YouTube, Instagram, and other platforms. Most of the old articles were all verbal content with one photograph at best. In addition, Ricardo had no exposure to surfing, so all the names of the various competitions, beaches, and events meant nothing to him. But he kept looking. He found various names of surfing champions from endless competitions categorized by year on

Wikipedia, but names without a picture were useless. What he was looking for was a photo with a name. If he could find Paul's true name, then Dan could run that through the FBI. Without a name, the only chance of finding Paul was if Paul made some stupid mistake directly in front of a Panamanian cop, and Ricardo didn't think that was likely to happen.

Late that afternoon, when Ricardo heard Alison downstairs in the kitchen, he decided to give up his fruitless search for the day. Alison met him at the bottom of the stairs, handed him a glass of chilled white wine, and kissed him.

"Get some good writing done, sweetheart?" she asked.

"Um, no. I spent the afternoon researching," he replied

"Researching?"

"Old surfing magazines, mostly. Looking for something that might identify Paul."

"Any luck?" she asked

"No, it's like looking for a needle in a haystack."

"Well, come here, let me show you what I've been working on," she said, and took his hand and led him into her studio.

Alison's studio was a huge white room with big windows on three of the sides, plus a skylight. The floor was covered with large plastic sheets, which were covered with old dried splotches and dribbles of paint. Two huge half-finished paintings were up on easels in the middle of the room. Ricardo had seen Alison's large canvas frames before—her painting style was big and colorful so she usually painted on five by eight foot canvasses. But these canvasses were enormous, at least 10 x 14 foot frames, so large she had to use three or four easels plus ceiling wire to hold them up so she could paint. The two paintings dominated the room, each with a step ladder in front of them.

"Oh my God," he said as he walked into the room.

"I'm working on a set. I call it Adam and Eve," she said.

There was a discernible male and female figure on each one canvas, but they were enveloped in swirling images and colors, totally symmetrical but at the same time wild and orgiastic. Each of the naked figures had Alison's stylistic soft, almost luminescent curves of flesh that dissolved into to color and swirls around the bodies.

"I love them!" Ricardo said.

"They're my first commissioned pieces," Alison said proudly. "A banker and his wife saw my elephant bone series and asked me to do an erotic biblical scene. I did a bunch of sketches, and they picked Adam and Eve."

"Unbelievable." Ricardo said as he stepped closer to examine each of the paintings.

"Yeah," Alison continued. "They came by a few days ago and really liked them."

"Is this for a bank?" Ricardo asked.

"No!" Alison laughed. "I don't think they would look right in a bank. No, they bought a big house outside of town and want art for it. I'm hoping that they'll commission some more pieces from me when I finish these."

"Wow, Alison. I'm speechless," Ricardo said.

Alison laughed, "Good. Then let's eat. Dinner's ready, and I'm starved."

*     *     *

Later that night, Ricardo and Alison were lying in bed. Sex had been good. It had been very good. Alison was feeling dominant and Ricardo was glad to let her take control. She held his arms down by the wrists and sat on his face rubbing her pussy back and forth over his mouth and extended tongue. She was very wet, and pussy juice dribbled into his mouth and down the sides of his face.

"Oh, God!" she said. "I don't want to come..." But she kept on rocking back and forth harder and harder. At times Ricardo found it hard to breathe. But he kept up with her, holding his tongue firm and extended so that it pressed against her clitoris as she moved forward, sliding it into her pussy and then rubbing against her clitoris again as she moved back.

"Oh God," she said again and again. He could tell when she was about to come because her clitoris softened, and the taste of her pussy changed. Then she came and juice poured out of her. She moaned and fell over on her side, grabbing his head and bending herself over him. They lay like that for a while. His tongue could still just reach her pussy and he would quickly touch and tease it with the tip of his tongue.

"Oh no," she moaned. "Sensitive..." She shifted her hips back just out of reach of his tongue. He had to content himself with licking at her public hair.

"God, I needed that," she finally said. "How are you doing?"

"Doing great," Ricardo said. "I didn't know you were a squirter," he teased.

"I am not!" She mockingly answered, and then asked, "Would you like to come?"

"Uh huh, yes, I would. No rush though, baby."

"Okay, baby," she said, shifting her body down so she could wrap her arms around him. Let me just hold you a bit."

She held him and they kissed lightly and nuzzled. For the first time since he had left Panama, he felt good. He could feel Alison's breasts against his side, and her thigh was resting across his thigh and just touching his cock. He breathed quietly and could feel her pulse. He began to think of all the times they had had sex, and how it was always good, how much he enjoyed the feel and smell of her body, the sound of her voice, her laugh. He felt his thoughts beginning to swirl around these images, memories, feelings, sounds, smells, and tastes. It was almost as if he was dissolving into her. He didn't want to do that, though. He tried to pull his thoughts back. That's when he realized his cock was getting hard.

"Hmm?" Alison said. She had noticed it too. "Oh, okay, baby," she said, and slid down the bed and began to suck on him. She kept one hand tight on the base of his cock while she sucked and licked the head, and used her other hand to play with his balls. He got harder still.

She turned and looked at him. There was a gleam in her eye.

"I want you to fuck me like a boy," she said.

"What?"

"Fuck me like a boy," she repeated. She kept her left hand tightly gripping the base of his cock while she reached over to the nightstand with the other hand, opened a drawer and pulled out a condom and a tube of lubricant. She used her teeth and her right hand to tear open the condom and quickly rolled it onto him. Still holding the base of his cock, she flipped the top of the lubricant open with her thumb, and squeezed out about two ounces of lubricant directly over his cock and rubbed it all around the condom.

"Are you sure?" he asked, "The last time we tried...."

"I've been practicing with a dildo," she interrupted, and turned over on her stomach and raised her hips.

Ricardo got behind her, used his fingers to wipe a glob of lubricant from the base of his cock and rub it around the rim and inside Alison's asshole. Then he slowly slid his cock into her, worrying that it would hurt her but loving how it felt. "Oh, yes," she said, "yes, yes..." He got it all the way in and began to stroke back and forth. "Oh yes, fuck me, fuck me," she moaned.

And he did. Harder and harder, until finally he came.

\*       \*       \*

Afterwards, when they were taking a shower together, wiping all the lubricant and love juices off their bodies, she said, "Fucking in the ass is messy, but I can see why you gay boys do it."

"I'm not gay," Ricardo retorted in a mock scolding way.

"Okay, let me rephrase that," she said. "I can see why all you metro-sexual liberated polyamorous bi-sexual tri-sexual gay boys do it."

Ricardo laughed, and then said, "Yeah, it's a thrill. A

ghastly thrill, but a thrill. We'll probably need to change the sheets."

*     *     *

Later, after changing the sheets, they were laying in bed, just talking.

"You know," she said, "you're pretty good for an older guy."

"Ha," he said. "Well, it's easy with you."

"Yeah," she said, and was quiet for a bit. Then she said, "You see, it's not so bad here."

"Uh huh," Ricardo said, and then asked, "Do you think it was the paintings?"

"What do you mean?"

"Do you think it was the paintings that got us so horny?"

"Adam and Eve?"

"Uh huh. They're pretty erotic."

Alison thought for a moment, "Well," she said, "that couple who ordered it, they said they wanted it real erotic. So, I guess I succeeded. But what I was saying is that it's not so bad here. I have my painting area. You could have that room for writing. I know you don't like the pressure. But I'm just saying if, for some reason, you can't ever go back to Panama, you could stay here."

Ricardo sat up in the bed and looked at her.

"Not ever go back to Panama? Hmm...I hadn't considered that possibility."

He lay back down, and frowned. He hadn't thought about that. He had paid Ted for the next month, but somehow simply assumed that, like some American TV show, they would capture Paul, and everything would return to normal. Even though he knew how inefficient the Panama police force was, he had not seriously considered the possibility that Paul might continue to simply be not found, for months, for years, forever... and that there would always be a risk that his own safety would be in jeopardy if

145

he returned. This was not a good thought.

Alison reached over and rubbed his chest. "Oh, baby," she said, "I didn't mean to upset you. I was just wanting to say you could stay here."

Ricardo placed his hand over hers, looked at her, and smiled. "Thank you, Alison. I do appreciate that. Let's see how things play out."

They both lay there, each wrapped in their own thoughts.

# Chapter 28: Beach Club Pupu

It wasn't until the fourth day of internet research that Ricardo hit pay dirt. In 1968, there was a surfing championship held at the Beach Club Pupu in Peru. Ricardo had given up counting the number of surfing contests that were held on various beaches each year in every country with an ocean. He was bleary-eyed from looking at all the California sites and old articles and had switched over to using the word "international" with all the surfing searches. On some site he found a reference to an old blog, and that blog kept an archive of stories, and he found a story about a young American surfer who had won first place at the Club Pupu in Peru in 1968, but had his trophy taken from him when he had threatened another surfer with a knife right before the awards ceremony. There was no picture in the blog but there was a name: Michael Skinner. The blog article stood out because it was the only one that Ricardo had come across that mentioned a weapon. In fact, it was the only one that mentioned any kind of violence. There had been many articles referencing drunken parties, wild antics, misdemeanor arrests for DUIs, etc., but no assaults. Ricardo spent another three hours using various combinations of search terms to include Michael Skinner, Club Pupu, Peru, arrests, lost trophy, championship, etc., this time looking for an image, all to no avail. Finally, he went back a few years and tried the name Michael Skinner with various words related to California, and finally found a listing for a 1967 California surfing contest that listed an M. Skinner from Jacksonville, Florida. But combining the name Michael Skinner with

Jacksonville did not produce any hits. But then, on a hunch, he simply typed in Jacksonville, Florida, and "yearbook", and found a high school in Jacksonville, Florida, that had their entire yearbooks online for 1965 through 1975. He picked 1966 to start, figuring that if Michael graduated from high school in 1966, he might have booked to California in 1967 for the surfing contest. He looked through the student photos under "S" in the 1966 yearbook, and there he found a student named Michael Skinner who he thought looked like a very young Paul. If he had seen the photo before knowing about the Peru incident, he might not have seen the resemblance. But it was there. The kid in the picture had longish hair, of course and was smiling. But there was something about the eyes and nose. Plus, the caption under his name read *Surfer Boy*.

Ricardo then spent another few hours trying all different search combinations, trying to find more pictures, but he had no luck. This one tiny 1966 high school yearbook photograph was all he could find.

Finally, late that afternoon, when his eyes were hurting from staring at the laptop screen trying to find pictures, he finally gave up and emailed Dan what he had found, including all his internet links, plus a screenshot of the picture of Michael Skinner.

He went downstairs feeling that at least he had done something. Maybe there was no relationship. Maybe it was just a resemblance and nothing more. Maybe the name Michael Skinner would lead to nothing. But at least he had tried. He felt that the rest of the investigation was out of his hands.

He got downstairs and found a note from Alison. "Had to run out. Be back in an hour." Ricardo smiled. It didn't say when she had left. He went to the refrigerator and took out a bottle of white wine they had opened the night before but had not finished. He poured a full glass, then on a whim decided to go into her painting room and look at those paintings again.

There was that familiar smell of paint as he opened the

door. The late afternoon light coming through the windows was a deep but fading yellow. He switched on the overhead lights, walked over to the paintings, stood there sipping on his wine, and looking at them. They were gorgeous, he thought. Alison's style, her colors, her craziness, her determination and her eroticism. She was talented, and he felt proud to know her. He stood there for a few minutes, looking back and forth at the two paintings, looking at the detail, looking at the emotions, and a strange sadness started to creep over him. If she was such a fantastic person, why did he always pull away? He remembered how, back in Panama, she had accused him of being able to commit to her for only two weeks at a time, and how those words had burned him. But it was true. And this trip was no different. He fled here because he needed refuge, but he never envisioned staying here for an indefinite period of time. The thought of it made him antsy.

He walked back to the door, switched off the light, closed the door gently behind him, and went into her living room. This was her space, her colors, her furniture, her arrangements. He sat down in a white leather easy chair near the window and continued thinking. He did feel like he loved her. But he had loved Eve just as intensely, and Haley before Eve, and others before Haley.

His cell phone beeped. It was an email from Dan, thanking him for the information and saying he would check it out first thing in the morning.

Ricardo went back to the refrigerator, poured another glass of wine and returned to the easy chair. Was it just his bad luck? Or was there something about his sexuality—bi, poly, or otherwise—that made it impossible for him to be happy with just one woman? Was he just selfish and spoiled and simply unwilling to do the hundreds of compromises necessary to make a relationship work? He didn't think that was it. After all, he had been married twice, and both marriages had lasted several years. So, he was capable of compromising, but maybe not, he thought, on a permanent basis. Or maybe it was that Alison was simply not someone he could live with for long periods of time. He thought about sex with her. The sex was great. She was a talented lover. When he was with her in bed, he wasn't fantasizing about some other woman or some other man. He was totally present with her alone. But he remembered that the same was true with Eve. For the few months that he and Eve were together, he thought he had found the greatest sex partner in the world. And the same was true with Haley before Eve. Great sex, even deep intimate emotional sex, sex that made him come back for more... all that still wasn't enough to make him stay. The only thing he could conclude was that he truly must be fucked up. What more could a guy want? He mentally ran through all of Alison's positive traits: her beauty, her intelligence, her artistic talent, her good business sense, her compatible sexual appetite and ethos, and how easy it was to talk with her... Then he thought about her negative traits: her moodiness, her temper that could flare up out of nowhere, her quick sharp tongue, and her preoccupation with her career... none of which, he thought, were any different than his own negative traits. Certainly, they were traits he should be able overlook when considering all her positive qualities. And yet, he didn't feel at home here. He just wanted to be back in Panama, in his tiny apartment with the heat, the ceiling fan, the writing desk, endless time to write, and no one to answer to. And now, that possibility was on indefinite hold. What was he going to do? He couldn't stay here for months waiting for them to find Paul. He had never planned for that. How long would he stay? How long *could* he stay? If he left, where would he go? The weight of the situation began to sink in on him. The more he thought about it, the more he realized how pissed off he truly was. He had cultivated the perfect life in Panama. And Paul had ruined it. Now, it was like Ricardo was the fugitive and Paul was doing what he wanted to do with total impunity. Fuck that shit.

"I'll give it one more week," Ricardo thought. "One more week here, and then I'm going back."

# Chapter 29: Complications

The next day around noon, Ricardo was sitting at the small table in Alison's meditation room emailing back and forth with his publisher when his cell phone rang. It was Dan calling him. Ricardo had expected to hear from Dan but had assumed he would communicate via email. So the phone call came as a surprise.

"Dan?" Ricardo asked. "What's wrong?"

"Nothing's wrong my man. I just wanted to call and thank you. That was good detective work. Paul *is* Michael Skinner."

"Really? Are you sure?"

"Absolutely. We ran that name through the FBI and found the warrant. It's a 1983 warrant out of California for a murder. He got arrested but jumped bail. We still gotta find him, but now we got fingerprints and a mug shot. Interesting dude. I got his whole history. Evidently, he got drafted in '69, well... first, he got arrested for draft evasion, but then they dropped that when he agreed to go into the service. And get this: they put him into army intelligence. He spent a year in Vietnam, until he picked up some shrapnel in his knee. That's how he hurt his knee—in Vietnam, not surfing. Then they put him stateside and had him doing undercover work infiltrating protest groups. Remember the Weathermen? He was an informant against them! He could have had a career in the Army. But he kept fucking up, getting into fights and stuff. Plus he kept having surgery on his knee. Eventually the Army booted him out. Evidently he decided to continue doing undercover work on his own. When he got busted in '83, the cops found almost a dozen fake passports, fake drivers' licenses, birth certificates, etc. He was doing identity theft decades before it was even called that. No one knows exactly what he was doing all those years with those different identities. But he sure wasn't working a regular job anywhere, so we assume he was involved in various frauds or scams."

"Wow!"

"Yeah! And let me tell you, José Fernando wants to buy you dinner when you come back. If José Fernando can catch this guy—an American wanted fugitive—he'll be a hero," Dan said with a laugh. "Or at least he thinks he'll be. He's already envisioning a show about him on American TV. He's cancelled every cop's vacation, and even their days off, and made them all drop every other case to find Paul. Or I should say, Michael Skinner."

Ricardo paused and then asked, "Do you think it's safe for me to come back now?"

Dan's intake of air was audible over the cell phone. "Hmm, I don't know, Ricardo. I mean, there is certainly more police activity now, so that's a plus... but this guy is still an unpredictable nutcase, and that hasn't changed. I would say you're better off staying in the States until we catch him. I mean, if you can stay away."

"I'd like to come back if I could," Ricardo said.

"Well, it's up to you, but I wouldn't advise it. Why don't you give it a couple more days? See if José Fernando's men can flush him out."

"Okay," said Ricardo. "I had already decided to wait one more week, so I'll do that. But send me updates, will you? You can just email me, but let me know what's going on."

"I will do that, sir," said Dan. "You take care up there, and I'll email you. Let me know what you end up deciding."

"Yeah, okay. Thanks for calling," Ricardo said.

"No, thank *you* for your work," Dan replied.

Ricardo hung up the phone and thought about the call. Maybe things were getting better step by step. Maybe he'd be able to go back to Panama soon after all. Maybe the police weren't all that incompetent. After all, now they were motivated, because they wanted their weekends and vacations back. He wanted to tell Alison, but he wasn't sure how to phrase it. They still hadn't talked directly about how long he might stay. Certainly the sex had been good. But no matter how good the sex was, thinking about staying for an extended period of time just gave him a knot in his stomach. He looked at his watch. Alison usually took a lunch break about now. He decided to go downstairs and talk with her.

She was on the phone in the living room when he walked downstairs. He went into the kitchen to refill his coffee mug, but he could hear her talking.

"No, that's not a good idea right now, Allen. I've got a friend visiting... No, no, well I don't know... He's an old friend from Panama. I told you about him... he writes down there... yes, that one... well, I don't know... no that's not a good plan right now... well, of course I do... look, can we talk about this later?... yes, I promise. I'll call later."

She hung up the phone and shook her head.

Ricardo walked over, sat down across from her, and said, "Problems?"

"No," she answered, "that was my friend Allen. He wanted to come up and visit."

"Oh, Ricardo said, "I see... competition. Tell me about him."

Alison frowned. "Well, there's not much to tell. I met him in Albuquerque a month or two ago. He runs an upscale gallery there. My agent had placed a couple of my paintings there on consignment a few months ago, and when they sold fast, Allen called me directly and said he wanted to do a show. You know, the usual. 'Meet the artist' stuff. So I sent him eight paintings and then drove down to meet him. It was a good show. I sold six of the paintings, which is a good percentage for me. Afterwards, he took me out to dinner."

"Uh huh..." said Ricardo, "and then?"

Alison shrugged. "Well, yeah, you know, one thing led to another. I think you'd actually like him. He's a lot like you."

"Well, in that case, I'd hate him. Good in bed?"

"Yeah, fuck you, but yeah, he's okay... he treats me nice. Shit, you know me. I like to be well treated."

Ricardo thought to himself. Yes, that was true. He did know her, and her openness about sex was, just like his own sexuality, a double-edged sword. She had no problem juggling one or two or even three lovers at a time. She was always brutally honest about that.

"Besides, his gallery is well-connected," she added. "He can sell a lot of my paintings."

"So he wants to come up for a visit?"

"Yeah."

"Is he bi?"

Alison looked at Ricardo, trying to determine if he was serious or just teasing her. "No, Ricardo. No, he's not."

"Just checking," Ricardo said with a smile. In fact, he could not imagine sharing Alison in bed. He too was guilty of liking attention. When he was in bed with her, she gave him her full attention. He was suddenly aware of an odd feeling. Here he was, about to tell her of progress in the search for Paul, feeling that he wanted to be in Panama and away from here, and yet, at the exact same time, feeling a bit jealous of the new guy Allen. Somehow, the idea of some other guy sliding right into the bed with Alison right after he left, if he were to leave, unnerved him, made him want to stay. At the same time, it made him doubt the sincerity of her offers that he stay. Just another reason he didn't like being in relationships, he thought to himself.

"Well," he said, "not to change the subject, but I just got off the phone with Dan." And he proceeded to update Alison as to the case, about Mike Skinner's history, about how José Fernando had increased the police patrols, about the 1983 warrant. But he left out the part where Dan had said that it wasn't safe to return yet, knowing that Alison would ask.

And it was her first question. "Did he think it was safe for you to go back?"

Ricardo decided to shade the truth. "Possibly," he said. "He wanted to wait a couple of days to see how frequently

José Fernando's men were patrolling around the Island."

"The what?" she asked.

"Oh, sorry," he said. "I've gotten into the habit of calling the apartment building the Island, after some comment you made about it being an island of misfits when you were there."

"Oh yeah, misfits, I remember that. I guess I was right about that," she said. "Listen, Ricardo, there's no need to rush back there. Why not wait until they capture this guy? He's murdered two people! There's no reason to go back until it's completely safe."

Ricardo tried to defuse her argument. "Well, it may be safe now. Dan will let me know now in a day or two. And besides, I don't want to stand in Allen's way."

"Fuck you," Alison said and frowned. "I'd like you to stay... besides, Allen's married."

"Really? Well, how does he... oh no, never mind, it's none of my business." Clearly, he was not defusing the discussion. He could tell she was getting irritated. "Are you hungry at all? Do you want to go get something to eat?"

"No... I was, but now I'm not. There's stuff in the refrigerator if you're hungry now. I'm going to paint for another hour or so, if you want to wait."

"Okay," he said. "I'll wait. I'd rather eat with you."

She went back into her painting room and closed the door. "Well," he thought ruefully to himself, "that went well." This was the problem Ricardo had with Alison: the other edge to her passionate side. She could get irritated as easily as she could get aroused. He hoped it would pass by the time she got hungry. He got up and went back upstairs to the meditation room.

There he looked at the emails from his publisher. His publisher was based in New York, but wanted to set up a book signing tour that would involve five cities in California, Oregon, and Washington. The tour he was proposing would take two months.

"No, I don't want to do that," Ricardo wrote. "I might be willing to do one city. Maybe San Francisco. I like San

155

Francisco."

"We're hitting better demographics in the Pacific Northwest," his publisher wrote back. "How about we set up signings in Seattle and Portland?"

"I don't know. Maybe one city," Ricardo wrote back. "But let me think on it for a day or two." He wanted to see what progress Dan made, or rather, what progress José Fernando made.

# Chapter 30: Nothing Furthers

But there were no new developments in Panama. Over the next three days, Ricardo talked or texted with Dan daily. José Fernando had distributed new flyers showing Paul's pictures from the ATM photo and from the 1983 warrant, but his men had found no trace of him. An analysis of the records at the bank in Villa Rosario showed that Paul actually had used several different ATM cards to withdraw cash, and none of those cards appeared to have been used again since he moved out of the Island. His men had taken to viewing videos from various ATMs in Panama City and La Chorrera to see if they could spot him, but they were having no luck. Dan continued to advise Ricardo not to come back just yet.

Worse, Ricardo seemed to be getting on Alison's nerves. Even when he gave her news that he would have thought would make her happy—that he wasn't sure he could go back to Panama just yet—she seemed irritated. Not angry, not hostile, just slightly irritated. It was little things, her way of disengaging bit by bit, laughing or smiling less every day. It was a pattern that he had gone through with her time and again, over several years. They were great lovers for about ten days, but at some point after two weeks, he seemed to get on her nerves, and he was already into his third week.

He made an extra effort to be nice. One afternoon while he was reviewing some files on his laptop, he ran across an old photograph of her that he always liked. They had been sitting at an outdoor restaurant, and she was leaning back from the table against the wall, checking her cell phone. It was the end of summer and she was very tan. It was sunset and the light glowed a dark red. She wore her hair longer back then, and strands of it had fallen in her face. The combination of her long dark hair, her dark skin, the reddish light, and the look on her face, made her look Italian. It was one of his favorite pictures of her. He looked at it for awhile, feeling soft towards her, and thinking how beautiful she was. That evening, after dinner, he showed her the photograph.

"Remember this?" he asked opening his laptop to the photo.

She glanced at it. "Oh, yeah." She didn't seem interested.

"It's one of my favorite shots of you."

"Hmm... yeah," she said looking away. "I've never liked it."

"Really?" he said. "I do. It's a great photograph. You're very photogenic."

"I hate it when people use that word," she said.

"Why? You're beautiful."

"That's not what photogenic means," she said. "Photogenic means that someone is not beautiful, but that they look beautiful in pictures. It means the opposite of being beautiful. People always say it when they they're trying to compliment someone, but it's not a compliment. It just means they photograph well."

"Well, I think you're beautiful."

"I'm not," she said. My face is not symmetrical. I'm not beautiful at all. My left eye is smaller than my right eye, and it's offset from my nose. Look at my left eye. See how it's smaller? And look at my jawline. See how it's bigger on this side? You like that photograph because it's taken from the left. That's my good side. But anything taken from my right looks horrible. My jaw's all out of proportion."

She pulled out her cell phone and scrolled through until she found a photograph of herself taken from the right side. "See here," she said. "See how my jaw line juts out. And look at my hairline." She pulled her hair back. "See how it's uneven."

"Well, Alison, no one's face is perfectly symmetrical," Ricardo said. "That's what makes them unique and beautiful."

"No, that's not true. You look at famous beautiful women. Their faces are perfectly symmetrical. That's one of the reasons they're beautiful."

Ricardo thought to himself that this discussion was going nowhere. She was being argumentative and refusing to take a compliment. Plus, he had clearly hit a nerve. She had obviously spent time examining her face and did not find it as beautiful as he did. He understood that she had a painter's analytic eye for things. But he thought she was just using that to gain some distance from him. He thought of that two-word judgment in one of the I Ching hexagrams: *Nothing furthers*. He put away his laptop and decided to drop the subject. But evidently Alison was not done talking about it.

"That's the problem with writers," she said, "You never see things as they are. You take these real world events—and I've read your stuff Ricardo; and I know this—you take these real world things and you rewrite them, you twist them to make them beautiful, or interesting, or provocative, By the time you're done, they don't resemble what really happened at all. You call it fiction, but I think it's really fabrication."

Ricardo felt his hackles go up. "Really?" he said, "how is that different from painting?"

"I paint what I see. I may add symbolism. I may connect it to an archetype, but I'm painting what I see. You take a real world event and twist it."

"That's bullshit, Alison," Ricardo says, "Writers write. Call it what you want, it's writing."

"No, that's not true. I remember reading about me in one of your books. What was that character's name? Oh yeah, Enid. Horrible name. You took whole conversations we had and stuck them in there, coming out of her mouth, and gave them a whole different context."

"Enid wasn't you," Ricardo said.

"Maybe not, but you put me in her. You took things I said and twisted them. That's not writing—that's plagiarism."

Ricardo was angry now, but saw no point in this argument.

"I write how I write... Besides, I always thought you liked that book. At least that's what you told me."

Alison looked down at the table. "I did like it," she said, "I'm just saying you don't see things as they are. It's our mutual occupational hazards. I have to look at things and see what they are, and try and capture their essence. You look at things and see something else. Like when you look at me and say I'm beautiful. You're not seeing me. You're not seeing me at all. I'm just going to end up as another woman in one of your books. Another ex-lover you pine over in your island of misfits when you're not out there fucking whores and strangers. But you're the misfit, Ricardo. I've told you this before. You don't want to grow up and be in an adult relationship."

"Well," Ricardo snapped, "I certainly don't want to be in an abrasive relationship."

"All relationships are abrasive, Ricardo," she snapped back. "You're supposed to work around that."

Alison was quiet for a minute. Ricardo sensed she was about to say more, so he remained quiet too. But she had no more to say. She got up and took her plate to the kitchen and said, "I'm going to go paint," and left the room.

After another day of feeling like he was in Alison's way, Ricardo called his publisher and told him to go ahead and arrange a book signing. His publisher picked Seattle. Ricardo then told Alison that his publisher was really pressuring him to do this signing and he felt he had to go. And so he went. It was just like Africa, he thought, two good weeks, and then crap. He remembered that it was after the Africa trip that he had vowed never to let a visit with Alison last over two weeks. And here he had broken his own rule. She drove him to the airport, kissed him goodbye nicely, but never asked if he was planning to come back.

# Chapter 31: Seattle

Ricardo's plane landed in Seattle that Friday afternoon. The sky was gray and raining. He took the light rail train from the airport to downtown Seattle, then walked to his hotel. On one hand, he was glad his publisher had picked Seattle. It was a city where it was easy to lose oneself, slip into the gray mist, become just another anonymous person in a coffee house or on the street. They called it the Northwest Chill, meaning that no one bothers anyone or interacts with anyone in Seattle. If Ricardo had to be away from home, Seattle is where he wanted to be. But that was the problem. It was hard to enjoy Seattle if one didn't feel that one had a home somewhere, and right now, Ricardo felt that he didn't have a home. His home in Panama was all up in the air, and it had been many years since he felt like he had a place he could call home in the States. He loved Alison, but her house was not his home, especially when she was moody or angry. He wasn't sure where he was going to go after Seattle, and his unknown future hung over him like the dismal skies above.

But in the meantime, there was work to be done. His publisher had scheduled three nights of readings and book signings for him: two in downtown Seattle, and one in Bellevue. The first reading was set for two days hence. For the two days before the first reading, Ricardo did several short radio interviews, promoting the readings, and spent hours arranging and rearranging the poems and excerpts he wanted to read. He omitted all the poems about Alison. He just didn't feel like reading those this trip. As usual, his publisher had someone to pick him up from the hotel and drive him to the reading. The first one was at a large bookstore in the Capitol Hill area. It seemed well attended, and there was wine for him to drink between poems, and for the forty-five minutes that he read, he felt glimmers of his old self: acerbic, witty, and poetic. Afterwards, he greeted people in the lobby at a small table, and signed copies of books that they had purchased.

His publisher always claimed that the publicity value of such readings and book signings lasted longer and far outweighed the number of books that were sold at the event. Ricardo didn't care. He was just glad to be doing something—anything—that took his mind off Panama, off Michael Skinner, and off Alison.

In the past at such events, Ricardo would keep his eye out for any attractive admirer, male or female, and chat with them at the signings. Occasionally, if he was lucky, he could entice them up to his hotel room—or occasionally they would insist on coming to his hotel room—and there would be several hours of gratuitous sex. Ricardo was always aware that this was akin to groupie sex—people who wanted to fuck him or be fucked by him, only because of the fact that he was, in their minds, famous. But that never stopped him from playing along.

But this trip was different. After reading, when he had to sit at the table in the lobby and interact with people, the feeling of being homeless in the world came back. He simply didn't feel like he wanted to be with anyone. It wasn't that he missed Alison so much. In fact he was pissed at her for being so difficult. But he just felt like his life was in such an uproar that it was impossible to feel sexy. So even though there were several attractive and engaging people at the book signing that first night, Ricardo remained somewhat formal with them: polite, considerate, but without flirting back. He returned to his hotel that night alone and glad to be alone. He had the driver stop along the way to buy a bottle of wine, which he drank alone that night in his hotel room.

Ricardo had requested that his publisher schedule an extra day between the first and second readings, because he wanted to see if he could track down Colin, an old friend. Colin had been a mentor of his years ago, several decades ago, in fact. He was an editor, at least fifteen years older than Ricardo, whom Ricardo had met years ago on the east coast, years before Ricardo had started writing his own books. But when Ricardo had started writing, he had turned to Colin for advice, and Colin had helped him, editing several of his books. He had encouraged him and had occasionally made love to him. Colin had retired from his job and moved to Seattle, where he lived alone and continued doing freelance editing. Ricardo always viewed him as a shining example of someone who lived his life on his own terms. Even in retirement, he was in high demand as an editor by publishers. Colin traveled the world and worked when he needed the money. Over the years, as Ricardo's books sold, he had kept in touch in Colin, via email or an occasional phone call. Colin was always someone whom Ricardo could turn to, not only for professional advice, but at times for personal advice. He remembered one time, ten or fifteen years ago, he had flown to Oaxaca, Mexico, to join Colin on a vacation. They shared a hotel room, made love, drank, ate at nice restaurants, and talked about life. Ricardo remembered one night at dinner at an outdoor restaurant on the zócala in the middle of Oaxaca, after several glasses of wine, Colin turned to Ricardo and said, "You know, you're not bad looking. You ought to find someone to settle down with while you're still young." At that point, Ricardo was in his early fifties, and Colin, he estimated, had to be in his late sixties, maybe even in his early seventies. When Colin had said that, Ricardo detected a note of sadness in his voice, and wondered if Colin had regrets about his life. Still, for his age, Colin looked good, and life to Ricardo back then seemed open and full of promises.

Ricardo thought about these memories as he searched for Colin's number. Ricardo had emailed him regularly from Panama over the past few years, but he realized it had been at least two years since they had last talked by phone. He found Colin's phone number and dialed it.

But someone else answered the phone. It seemed to be an Asian voice, judging from the accent.

"Uh, yes, is Colin there?" Ricardo asked, thinking that maybe he had dialed wrong.

"He is sleeping now," came the response.

"Okay... This is a friend of his... my name is Ricardo... who are you?" Ricardo asked.

"I am the caretaker," came the heavily accented reply. "Colin is asleep right now. He just ate, and now he is asleep."

"Okay..." Ricardo said, "Um, can you tell him that Ricardo called and that I will call him tomorrow?"

"Yes, I will write that down..." and there was a pause... "How do you spell that?"

Ricardo spelled his name and then asked, "Is he okay?"

"Oh yes. He just ate, and now he is asleep."

"Okay, tell him I will call tomorrow."

"Yes, I will tell him."

Ricardo hung up and thought about this. He calculated the years. It was possible that Colin was in his early or mid-eighties by now. Ricardo knew that he had suffered a very minor stroke a few years back, but he seemed to bounce back from that fine. It had had no effect on his speaking or his wit. But still: a caretaker? Ricardo was concerned.

The next morning after breakfast at the hotel, Ricardo called Colin's number. Again, someone other than Colin answered, but this time it was a female voice.

"Oh, hello," Ricardo said, "Is Colin there?"

"Yes, who's calling?" the voice asked.

"This is Ricardo... I'm a friend of Colin's. Is he there?"

"Yes, just a minute."

Ricardo heard muffled voices.

The female voice came back on the line. "Just a minute," she said.

"And who are you?" Ricardo asked.

"I'm the caretaker," the female voice said.

Ricardo thought to himself: *So now we have an evening caretaker and a daytime caretaker... He has caretakers around the clock. That's not good.*

He heard Colin's voice come on the phone. "Hello?" Colin said.

"Hello Colin," Ricardo said, "this is Ricardo."

"Who?"

"Ricardo."

He heard Colin say to someone, presumably the caretaker, "I can't hear him." Then Ricardo heard the caretaker say, "Ricardo. His name is Ricardo."

Colin's voice came back on the phone.

"Oh yes, Ricardo, how are you?"

"Well, I'm fine. I'm in Seattle for a book signing. How are you?"

"Are you back? Back from wherever?" Colin said.

"From Panama. Just for a few days, yes," said Ricardo.

"Yes, well good, good. How is Panama?"

"It's fine," Ricardo said. "How are you?"

"What?" and then Ricardo heard Colin address the caretaker again. "I can't hear him."

"Can you hear me now?" Ricardo shouted into the phone.

"Oh yes, that's better."

"Well, I'm in Seattle and I was just calling to say hello," Ricardo shouted.

"Yes, well, thank you so much," said Colin, "Yes, thank you for calling, well, take care, goodbye."

And then there was some fumbling noises and muffled sounds and then the phone was hung up.

Ricardo sat there on his hotel bed, with the phone in his hand. He felt extremely sad. He tried to remember how Colin had looked, that night in Oaxaca, sitting at the table drinking wine. Was it ten years, or was it fifteen years ago? He wasn't sure. And yes, Colin had looked older then, and yes, Ricardo thought, we all age, but still... was this how it always ended up? Caretakers? Everything fading away? Ricardo wondered if he would end up this way. Even though Colin had already hung up, Ricardo pressed the "end call" icon on his cell phone. He put the phone on the bed and went into the bathroom and splashed water on his face, and came back and sat down by the bed. Yes, he thought, this is how it all ends up. He recalculated Colin's age again... yes, Colin could be in early eighties by now. And it wasn't the content of his responses. It was the far-away sound of his voice that haunted Ricardo. He was already gone. Ricardo thought back to all their times drinking or working on projects or just talking. And he felt immensely sad.

He looked back though his poems and found ones that in some way referenced Colin and he inserted them into the list of what he would read that night. At least he could memorialize his friend in his own way.

The reading that night went rather robotically. He got through it and when the driver was taking him back to the hotel, he made him stop, as he had after the first reading, but this time he bought two bottles of wine.

## Chapter 32: The Nature of Change

The next day, Ricardo slept in, woke around noon and ordered a late breakfast from room service. Just as he was finished eating, his cell phone rang. Ricardo picked it up. It was Dan.

"Hello, Ricardo, how are you?"

"I'm okay, Dan. How are you?"

Ricardo resented these little pleasantries because he knew that Dan would not be calling him if it wasn't something important.

"I'm fine, thanks," Dan said, "I have news for you."

"Yes?" Ricardo said, and thought, *yes let's get to it.*

"Well, I don't know where to start... Paul, or Michael Skinner, is dead."

Ricardo felt a shock wave hit him. "What? Really? What happened?"

"It's a long story. Have you got a second?" Dan asked.

Yes, of course," Ricardo said, sitting down in his hotel room chair. "Tell me everything."

"Okay. Well, it appears that Paul, or Michael, hell—I'll just call him Paul. He was staying in the area. We still don't know where, but he was apparently stalking Ted. I guess he wanted to kill him as well, and he might have gotten away with it, but he chose the wrong place. I'm speculating here, but I think that Paul thought that he was following Ted to a brothel, and he tried to abduct him outside the brothel entrance. But he was at Jenny's, and Jenny came out and shot Paul and killed him."

"Wait a minute," said Ricardo, "Ted was going to Jenny's brothel and Paul attacked him there?"

167

"Well no, Ted was going to see his wife."

"I don't understand."

"Ted's wife is Jenny," said Dan.

Ricardo was silent for a second.

"Jesus...okay, okay. So, Ted was going over to Jenny's place of business?"

"Right."

"And Paul attacked him?"

"Yes," said Dan. "In front of Jenny's door. Tried to cut his throat, almost succeeded, but Ted's a tough old dude. Then, Jenny comes out with a gun and shoots Paul."

"Jenny shot Paul?" Ricardo asked in a daze.

"Shot him four times, at least. We're still awaiting the autopsy. But definitely killed him."

"Dan... You're not shitting me, are you?"

"No."

"When did this happen?"

"Last night."

"Okay, okay... so, how's Ted? Ted's married to Jenny?" Ricardo still couldn't believe that.

Dan laughed a bit. "Yes, Ted is married to Jenny. That's a long story, for another time. But Ted's okay. He's in the hospital. Paul cut him pretty bad, but he'll be okay."

"Uh, Dan, are guns legal in Panama? I mean, is Jenny in any trouble?"

"No one is going to prosecute her, believe me. She's a hero. José Fernando is happy, although he would have preferred capturing Paul himself."

"Wow... I need some time to absorb all this... but this means I can come back, right?"

"Yup."

"...Can you explain it to me all again? So I can be sure that I'm not dreaming?"

"Of course." And Dan explained how Ted and Jenny had been married for a long time, and it was well known in the Panameño community, but nobody talked about it, and how, for a number of reasons, Ted lived at the Island apartment while Jenny ran her business, but how they raised their children well, and always went to church together, and how on certain nights Ted would come by Jenny's establishment and take her out to dinner, and on this particular night, as he approached the front door, Paul lurched out from the bushes, and grabbed Ted from behind, and tried to cut his throat, but Ted threw himself backwards on top on Ted, yelling and grabbing Paul's knife hand with one hand and reaching back and clawing at Paul's face with the other hand. The commotion caused Jenny to rush to the front door, and seeing Ted bleeding and struggling with Paul on the ground, pulled out a small .22 pistol from her waist and stood there, just a few feet away and aimed at Paul's head and pulled off two rounds, hitting Paul directly in the head. And then, to be sure, she shot him two more times. According to Dan, Jenny was a good shot, and everyone in town, at least all the Panamanians, knew she carried a gun and knew how to use it.

After Dan explained it again, Ricardo said, "I can't believe it. So Ted's going to be alright?"

"Uh huh. He's going to need some time to heal, but he's going to be okay."

"And I can come back?"

"I don't see any reason why not."

"Okay... okay... okay... I don't know how to thank you enough, Dan."

"I didn't do much," Dan said. "Why don't you come on home?"

"Yes, home... Yes, I think I will. Thank you again."

And he hung up.

He sat in the chair for several minutes. *Sweet Jesus,* he thought.

Then he got up and opened his laptop and started looking for flights back to Panama. "Just let me get through this last reading in Bellevue, and then I'm out of here," he said to himself.

## Chapter 33: Return to Panama

The next thirty-six hours went by in a blur: After Dan's phone call, Ricardo booked a flight back to Panama, selected his material for that night's reading, emailed his publisher not to schedule any more readings, somehow got through the reading in Bellevue that evening, got back to the hotel, packed his clothes and caught an early morning flight back to Panama City, and then a bus to Villa Rosario. With the flight time, including a two-hour layover in Phoenix, and a three-hour layover in Dallas, and the bus time, he didn't arrive back to his apartment until 8:00 p.m. After he unpacked and sat down on the bed, Ricardo realized how exhausted he was. He lay down in his clothes, fell asleep and didn't wake up until twelve hours later.

That next morning, Ricardo brewed coffee and took a cup out to his balcony, and sat at the small table there and took in the view. There was the skyline, blue with white clouds over the rolling hills surrounding Villa Rosario. There was the big palm tree over the picnic table in the patio area below where he and Gregg and Carl and Dan and Ted, occasionally Darren, and sometimes Jonathan, would sit and drink. Seeing it all again, he couldn't help but think that Alison had been right: it was a group of misfits... renegades, twisted killers, expats, sexpats, outlaws, and lost souls. And she was right about another thing: that group included him. Despite Gregg's murder, and Luciano's murder, and the attempt on Ted's life, Ricardo felt at home here. He fit in. He was a misfit in the U.S. where he never felt like he fit in, but here he felt he could be himself. And if that self included being pansexual, irresponsible, and unwilling to commit, well then, he was in good company. And as he sat there thinking about Alison, he also realized, with a frown, that in the midst of his being pissed at her and rushing to fly back to Panama, he hadn't emailed her to tell about Paul's death and his return to Panama. As far as she knew, he was still doing readings in Seattle. He needed to let her know. He wasn't feeling angry at her any more. He knew how she needed her space—so did he. The fact that he was living at her house for almost three weeks had to be annoying to her. No wonder she had to create some distance. She had given him refuge, no questions asked, when he needed to get out of Panama. He should have predicted that two weeks would be the most contact either of them could handle. It had always been that way between them. He loved her in his own way, and she loved him in her own way. We can't help our defects, he thought to himself, or the fact that our tolerance for other people can have such defined limits. We should be grateful for the little love that we can give to each other.

He took his coffee cup and went inside to his writing desk. He opened his laptop and composed a long email to her, apologizing for not writing sooner, and updating her as to Paul's death and his return to Panama. He had some difficulty trying to figure out how to explain his decision to fly straight back to Panama. It was as if a part of him felt that he should have flown first to Santa Fe, as if that's what people in relationships are supposed to do: stop by and see each other before going home. He wondered if she would feel hurt or slighted by the fact that he went straight to Panama. But he told himself that was just some kind of cultural "couples-think", and that Alison wouldn't have expected him to do anything he didn't want to do.

He told her as much as he knew about Jenny shooting Paul. He hadn't seen Dan yet, so the only information he had was what Dan had told him on the phone. It was obvious that he was safe in Panama now that Paul was dead, but he went ahead and said that anyway.

Somehow, at the end of the email, he was feeling a tenderness towards her. They had known each other for so many years, always running hot and cold, always having those same arguments. But damn, when it was good between them, it was good. He decided to end the email by saying that she was welcome to come to Panama soon to visit him.

He hit the Send button and got up to refill his coffee cup. Then he went back outside to his little balcony chair to enjoy the morning while it was still cool outside. As he sat down, he heard Dan coming up the stairs.

"Ah, you're up," Dan said when he saw him. "I heard you come in last night, but I figured you needed to crash."

"Yeah, man, I was exhausted," Ricardo said.

"I bet. It's been an exhausting month. You got any coffee left?"

"Yeah, I do. I've got sugar but no milk," Ricardo said, standing up.

"No, I take it black," Dan said.

Ricardo stepped inside his apartment to get Dan some coffee, and Dan sat down at the small balcony table in front of Ricardo's apartment. Ricardo came out, handed Dan his coffee and took his own seat at the table.

"So," said Ricardo. "Fill me in. What's happened since we talked?"

"Well, let's see," Dan said. "Ted is probably getting out of the hospital tomorrow. Paul cut his neck pretty bad, but missed the main arteries. Still, Ted had to have surgery. I visited him yesterday. He's doing okay. He's going to spend a week at Jenny's so that she can help him recuperate. What else? The police are downplaying the fact that Jenny is the one who shot Paul. They're trying to keep her name out of it. It's bad for La Chorrera's image to admit they have brothels here." Dan gave a little laugh. "Besides, most of the cops frequent that place and they didn't want that attention, either. They basically told the newspapers that the police shot Paul. It's funny reading the papers the last few days. One of them even claimed that there had been a blazing

173

gun battle between the police and Paul. That was funny. José Fernando's feeling pretty good. He came through this thing without having his name tarnished and without the police looking bad, and you know how rare that is. The papers really latched onto portraying Paul as some type of Satan...not so much because he killed Gregg, but because he killed that kid, who they're painting as a young student with a future."

"Fuck that, Dan. That kid was a hustler, just taking Gregg's money for blowjobs," Ricardo blurted.

"Yeah, I know that, and you know that. But that story doesn't sell papers. The murder of innocent children sells papers, so that's the story. You know what's weird though?"

"What?"

"Well, I still can't get a handle on who the fuck Paul, or Michael Skinner, was. I mean, I don't know anything more about him now than I did when you identified him and we found that warrant out of California. This was a guy with no past, no traceable means of support, no history, no passport, nothing. It makes me very suspicious. Mostly because he was working for military intelligence, and they have just clammed up completely. I even called a friend of mine in the FBI, and he couldn't find out anything else. It's like we can kind of follow him until the 1983 warrant comes out, and then nothing, zip, nada. I mean, that's really strange. You know, we live in such a connected age electronically, where everyone leaves a trail. I could get online and make a few phone calls, and in a couple of hours, I could tell you everything you've done this year, where you went, what you bought, who you were with. But with Paul, there is nothing. Maybe, maybe he left the states in '83, came down here, and managed to stay off the grid ever since. It's possible. But where did he get his money? That's the thing that bugs me. I convinced José Fernando to continue investigating the financial side, to issue more subpoenas. I told him that there might be an international money laundering ring he might uncover and be even a bigger hero. But it's weird. Paul lived here in Panama for at least seven years. That still takes a lot of money. And he wasn't from a rich family."

"Extortion?" Ricardo said, "Maybe he was blackmailing someone?"

"I just don't know. But one thing is for sure, I'm glad he's dead. I know you're against the death penalty and all, but from my point of view, some people just need to be killed. And he was one of them."

Both men sat quietly for a few minutes. Finally Dan said, "Are you going to stay here?"

"Yeah," said Ricardo, "I was planning on it. I like it here."

"Well, I think you'll find it interesting. I think Ted and Jenny are going to make some changes here, but they like you. Especially Jenny, she thinks you're okay, especially since you were the one who identified Paul as Michael Skinner. So they'll probably let you stay."

"What kind of changes?" Ricardo asked.

"Oh, you'll see. But I think you'll be pleased."

"Okay... do you think any the others will come back?" Ricardo asked, gesturing to the empty apartments on the second floor, but then added, "Shit, who's even left?"

"I doubt it any of the survivors will come back. I ran into Darren a few days ago. He and that Barbara woman are talking about getting married. Carl's back in the States, licking his wounds. He won't come back. He doesn't have what it takes to be an expat. Jonathan will stay in Panama because he likes the sex, but he won't come back to live here. He's a big talker but he's basically a chickenshit. Besides, I don't think Ted would rent to him again. Ted did get an email from Louis a few weeks back, saying he wasn't coming back. He bought some condo in Costa Rica and wired Ted some money asking him to ship his belongings there. I don't think he even knew about the murders. That's it buddy, it's just you, me, and Ted. The rest are gone or dead."

"Shit," was all Ricardo could say.

"Hey, that's life," Dan said. "Nothing ever stays the same. Speaking of which, I got things to do. Thanks for the coffee. See you later."

After Dan left, Ricardo sat on the balcony for a few more minutes, looking at the picnic table on the patio below, and remembering some of the good nights he had enjoyed there. But of all the nights drinking with the guys there, the best memory he had was that one evening when he and Alison sat there, drinking beer and just talking. After a few minutes, he stood up and went inside. There was no food in the apartment, so he decided to take a shower and walk into town to get some breakfast.

As he stepped out of the shower and was drying himself, he heard the tiny bell of his laptop ring, indicating email. He wrapped the towel around him and went over to his writing desk and looked. It was from Alison. He sat down and read it.

She wrote: "Thanks for the email and the update. I was going to write you and see how you were doing. You know I've always cared about you, Ricardo. I'm glad you're where you want to be and that you are safe. It's a horrible story. All that death. But maybe you can write about it. As for the invitation, thanks, but Allen is taking me to New York for a couple of weeks to show my paintings at a very uptown gallery. This could be a whole new level of exposure for my work. At least, I hope so. Keep in touch and be safe. Love, Alison"

Ricardo read it a couple of times and gave an involuntary shake of his head. He thought of Dan's words earlier that morning: "Nothing ever stay the same." But no, he thought. That's not quite true. Things change, but they mostly stay within certain patterns, like moons circling planets, always in a different place in the sky but always on the same path. He closed his laptop and went back to the bathroom to finish drying off.

He walked downtown, found a small café with outside tables and ordered huevos, rice and beans, some fried plantain, and some more coffee. While he ate, he watched the people walking up and down the street, and the cars and the horse-drawn carriages go by. Here's something that doesn't change, he thought. Everything looked exactly the same as when he first moved here. Maybe that was one of the reasons he liked this town. It was ironic, he thought, that one of the reasons he had originally moved here was that Villa Rossario had the reputation of being a safe town. It didn't turn out that way, but maybe now, things could be that way again.

On the way back to the Island, he stopped by the grocery store to get some supplies. Alejandro was there, and seemed glad to see him.

"Mi amigo, it's good to see you," Alejandro said. "When did you get back?"

"Just last night," Ricardo said.

"You left fast," Alejandro said. "I was worried I would never see you again."

"It was crazy, wasn't it?"

They talked about the murders, and about the publicity. Alejandro seemed dismayed at how the papers had portrayed Luciano. "I always said that boy was no good. I knew he would have an unhappy ending," he said to Ricardo. "You can't sell your soul for money without consequences."

"True," Ricardo said. "Very true."

They talked a while longer until some customers needed Alejandro's attention. They parted, promising to do dinner soon.

Ricardo bought some groceries and carried them back to the Island.

As he walked up the hill to the front gate, he saw a moving truck parked in front. *Now what?* he thought.

He walked through the front gate. Several workers were busy carrying boxes from the truck into different

177

apartments. He saw several women, some familiar looking, each standing in the doorway of the different first floor apartments, telling the workers where to put the boxes. *What the fuck?*" he wondered, and climbed the stairs to second floor.

Dan was standing there talking to Jenny, who turned and smiled and nodded towards him.

"Good morning, Jenny," Ricardo said in Spanish. "How are you?" He put his grocery bag down and gave her the customary Spanish kiss on the cheek.

"I am well, don Ricardo, how are you?"

"I am well, also. Much activity downstairs."

"Yes, don Ricardo, I am moving some of my girls in here. I want them in one place where I can protect them."

Ricardo stared at her, and then at Dan. Dan was trying hard not to grin. "It's true, Ricardo. She had been urging Ted to do this for years. Now seemed like a good time."

Ricardo looked back at Jenny, but before he could speak, Jenny said, "I know what you are thinking, don Ricardo. No, this will not be a brothel. My business is in La Chorrera, and business is good there. And I have new girls, but they all live in different apartments in La Chorrera. They are not always safe there, you know. These apartments were empty. I can rent to them cheaper than they would pay for apartments in La Chorrera. They can live normal lives here. If they work out for me, I will move them to La Chorrera. In the meantime, they have a nice furnished place to live. It works out well all around."

"Wow" was all Ricardo could say.

"But I have new rules here, don Ricardo. I will not rent to men here. Only you and this one," she said, pointing to Dan. "You two are good men. You can stay. Rent is the same. But this is not a brothel. You do not do any business with the girls here. You want a girl, you must come to La Chorrera, understand?"

"Yes, yes of course," Ricardo said.

"And you do not tell anyone in town where these girls

178

work."

"Of course not," Ricardo said.

"It is our little secret," said Jenny. "If everyone behaves, this will be a nice place to live."

"I promise," said Ricardo.

"Good," said Jenny. "And to be sure, I put someone next to you to make sure you behave."

"Oh?" said Ricardo and turned and looked towards his apartment. There, standing in the doorway of the apartment next to his, was Magali. She was smiling sweetly and gave him a little wave. He smiled and waved back. Then he looked back at Jenny. She was smiling. "You be nice to her," she said, "You know I'm a good shot."

"So I've heard."

"Okay, my husband will be back in a few days. Until then, Dan is in charge. Any problems, you let me know."

And with that, Jenny went downstairs. Ricardo just looked at Dan. "Jesus fucking Christ, Dan. This place is so fucking weird!"

"Ha, you said it. You'd better put your groceries away."

"Oh yeah."

He picked up his bag and walked over to his apartment door and dug out his key. Magali was still standing there, smiling at him.

"You live here?" She asked as if she didn't know.

"Yes, would you like to come in?" he asked.

"Just for a minute," she said. "The movers are bringing my boxes."

Ricardo carried his grocery bag in and placed it on the small table in the kitchen.

"Oh this is a nice apartment," Magali said.

"Well, they're all the same. Yours is nice too."

"Yes, big bed," she said, as she sat down on it and bounced a few times to test the firmness.

"We'll have to try it out," Ricardo said.

Magali just smiled. She pointed at his writing desk. "I don't have a desk that big."

"That's where I write," he said.

"What do you write?" she asked.

"Well... that's a long story," he said. Ironic words, he thought. And then Alison's email flashed through his mind, where she suggested, for the second time, actually, that he write about this place, about this apartment building and its misfit inhabitants.

"I write love stories," he said.

"Oh good," she smiled. "I *love* love stories."

*—FIN—*

# ABOUT THE AUTHOR

Robert Rahula was born in Spain to an American father and Spanish mother, but grew up in Virginia on the farm of his paternal grandparents. He returned to Menorca, Spain, in the 1960s to pursue his writing career. These days he travels in Europe, Central and South America for several months a year, giving readings and lectures, and spends the rest of his time writing, dividing his time between Spain and the United States.

Over the past 30 years, Robert has published dozens books of prose and poetry in Spain and in the United States. While he remains relatively undiscovered in the United States, he is revered in Spain as the founder of the "portilla" style of popular Spanish poetry: non-metered fluid verse that deals with love, loss, bisexuality, separateness, and growing older.

Selections of his poems, along with his blog on writing and his tour itinerary, appear on his Facebook page and on his website robertrahula.com. Readings of his poems can also be found on YouTube.

www.ingramcontent.com/pod-product-compliance
Lightning Source LLC
Chambersburg PA
CBHW071518100726
47908CB00004B/1206